BLEAK FRIDAY

·

AXEL HASSEN TAIARI
KELBY LOSACK
LYDIA XYTHALI
JO QUENELL
VIOLET LEVOIT

A KING SHOT PRESS BOOK

kingshotpress.com

King Shot Press
P.O. Box 80601
Portland, OR 97280

Cover design © 2020 Matthew Revert
www.matthewrevert.com
Typeset by Michael Kazepis

ISBN 978-1-7321240-7-3
Printed in the United States of America and worldwide

And together we sashay
Through variations of hell
A SILVER MT. ZION

RUINATION V.0.5 (BETA)
Axel Hassen Taiari

Reality's too brittle, so believe *this* because every word is true, and every word has power. Peep Ismat. It's Saturday night in the southern Parisian hood, so you know he's looking fresh—Heems circa *Wild Water Kingdom* hair with the young undercut, black bomber jacket, black drop-crotch pants, Ukrainian combat boots, and a blunt in his mouth. Leaning against a crumbling wall, cheetah-in-the-grass shit. Graffiti over the shoulder, dripping red: *FUCK THE PIGS*. Ismat wrote that. Now he's uploading a selfie about it—let the likes bloom. Too close to not fear a shot yet too far for a good shot: cop cars shriek and light up the night red and blue. The date: February 27th, 2018. Shit's real. A few weeks prior, Italian politician Luca Traini went on a two-hour shooting spree in Macerata and wounded six people of African descent. A few weeks later, far-right activists from Group Union Défense (GUD) armed with crowbars burst into a Parisian high school, started tossing bricks and chairs and rocks, crowbarred a student in the knee, and threw the usual salute before bouncing.

The thing is, Ismat doesn't know any of this and even if he did, the fuck is he supposed to do about it? He wasn't there, he isn't there, he won't be there. Man, that social media feed is poppin' tho.

Ismat's cool: a self-corrupting cyborg, core components a brainstem and haemal arch spilling over into the *there* via digioccult bdelloid processes masquerading as services. Ismat dumps daily shit into the ether (this isn't new—see cave paintings) but the ether mostly spits back garbage (on a human scale, this is new. The ether's got an owner now.) Don't trust these words, believe the words of a man who did hard time for armed robbery:

> The exteriorisation of memory and knowledge in the hyperindustrial stage is both what extends their limitless power and what allows them to be controlled. This control is now exercised by the cognitive and cultural industries of societies of control which regulate neurochemical activity and the sequence of nucleotides . . . . All this fully sets in place the question of a biopolitics of memory.[1]

---

[1] Steigler, Bernard. '*Anamnēsis and Hypomnēsis:* The Memories of Desire.' In Arthur Bradley & Louis Armand (eds), *Technicity.* 2009.

Biopower, cyberpower, necropolitics—perfect for the demonocracy. Divination's junk when prey invite predators over for dinner. Chronomancy's time stamps and metadata, a cute filter that displays the local time in case Ismat wanna feel empowered about it. Pendulum dowsing? Ismat's (*their*) tech screams his (*our*) location. Infinite knowledge in return, right?

Okay: Heather Heyer. Ricky John Best. Taliesin Myrddin Namkai-Meche. Micach Fletcher. Richard Collins III. Timothy Caughman. Srinivas Kuchibhotla. Alok Madasani. Then: Jamar Clark. Jordan Edward. Alton Sterling. Walter Scott. Eric Garner. Rekia Boyd. Michael Brown. Laquan McDonald. Akai Gurley. Tamir Rice. Philando Castile. Freddie Gray. Eric Harris. William Chapman II. Sam Dubose. Jeremy McDole. Ricky Ball. Keith Lamont Scott. And: CeCe McDonald. Justin Goodwin. Carl Joseph Walker-Hoover. Lateisha Green. Angie Zapata. Akyra Monet Murray. Kimberly Morris. Anthonio D. Brown— among so many others.

Too many.

These names pop up on Ismat's $900 palm-sized prosthesis. Some ring a bell, some don't. "The fuck?" says Ismat. He tries to swipe the names away—no go. He decides to GϕϕGΓƐ a few. Some don't lead to anything. Others are tied to ʏʋcƐbɘɘʏ and T¦ηʏƐɖη profiles. It's smiling faces and resumes and blogs and pictures.

Nothing odd. This is reality now. 2018 degaussed.

"Huh, all right," mutters Ismat, and reboots his device. The screen goes dark and—

•

A hackerspace off the grid. The air inside reeks of contraband Gauloises smuggled from Maghreb and empty beer bottles. Adriana Netrebska is alone, hunched over a backlit mechanical keyboard spewing electric red. Hood up, buds in the ear, Refused's *The Shape of Punk to Come* blasting loud enough to wreck a common mortal's eardrums. Keyboard's wired to an aging desktop. USB key plugged in, TAILS booted up, Vim running full-screen. Earlier that day, she sent plans for an upcoming protest in Paris, informed the locals of what the pigs were up to, where they were most likely to gather up, where riot chokepoints were drawn up, and how to proceed. Now, she writes, saying:

The Shape of Cypherpunk Yet To Come

You lazy motherfuckers. All of you reading this. Even my comrades. Especially my comrades. Every bit of your tech belongs to someone else. It's pre-colonized, pre-gendered, pre-corrupted, designed from the ground-up to betray you— to betray all of us. The original cypherpunk manifesto said it a quarter of a century ago:

We must defend our own privacy if we expect to have any. We must come together

What have we been doing since then? We've
been fucking ourselves up with each new shiny
toy dangled before us. We've let megacorps sell
us the same cyberpunk dystopia our half-assed
prophets envisioned. The owners made retro
chic. Threw glitter to cover up the warning
signs. They made oppression appetizing. If this
gains any traction, some of you reading this will
be hacktivists. Some will be activists. Some will
be people who don't know anything about tech
but know that big tech companies are evil. I
don't mean that casually. I mean blood-sacrifice-
evil. Rotten-to-the-core evil. Every act of digital
convenience is an act of surrender. Worse: you
surrender others. You snitch on us all. You are
complicit. I am not telling you to use Arch
Linux or airgap your computers or trawl your
Open-DDRT router's logs for signs of intrusion.
This literacy isn't needed.

I am not a luddite. Keep using tech but fight
at every turn using the oppressors' own tools.
Search. Find out how. It's all out there for now.

---

[2] Hughes, Eric. A Cypherpunk's Manifesto. https://www.activ-
ism.net/cypherpunk/manifesto.html. 1993.

Do it while there's still time. I am begging you. Do it while search engines spit back a modicum of truth. Turn your devices into pitchforks. Film the pigs. Film the fash. If you're gonna use those platforms at all, at least use them with a purpose. If we can't take them down, let's take them over. Reverse their orchestrated datamoshing.

Every picture you upload is a gift to them. Every word you speak or write while standing in their temples is an offering. You should feel guilty and ashamed every time you hand yourself over. You strengthen their sick rituals. These words should haunt you the same way our technology is haunted.

Revolt with every keystroke. Please.

Adriana Netrebska does not proofread her message. She posts on Reddit and 4chan and Twitter and Mastodon. She sends copies to Activism.net and uploads a backup to a server tied to junk info, hosted on a dusty Celeron in a Ukrainian bar.

"How deluded," says a voice behind her after the message is dispatched. Adriana moves—too slow.

The figure slits her throat. As she collapses, the figure whispers, "Scream *oxi* all you want, but we control the schema."

The killer takes its time while she bleeds out, pouring gasoline around the room and humming a mournful tune. It drags her by the hair to the center of the room and uses her blood to draw slithering symbols. When it is done, it opens the door and lights a match. The figure stands there, white robes flowing in the wind, staring at the match. Finally, it kneels, and let the flames do their job.

Adriana's message is read by less than thirty people. Activism.net never picks it up. It receives three upvotes on Reddit and nearly seven-hundred downvotes. Twitter locks her account. One 4chan user writes "lulcuck" and attaches a deepfake .gif of Stalin passionately making out with Obama. Search engines never index the website. Her Mastodon instance crashes six hours later. Her warning to the Parisian activists, although she would never know it, saves two lives.

•

Wolfenstein II: The New Colossus is the latest entry in the *Wolfenstein* series. This installment, like its predecessors, is a video game that invites the players to kill Nazis. There's a cool story there, and a charismatic protagonist called B.J. Blazkowicz—a Jewish-Polish American vet—and the ragtag resistance that rises to kill Nazis with him, but the narrative pales in comparison to the sheer fun of killing Nazis. Because that is really the centerpiece of this first-person shooter: killing all the Nazis. The developers fully leverage the series' alternate history setting (in which Germany won the war by pilfering high-tech weapons from the Da'at Yichud, a mystical Jewish society) and send the player to kill Nazis in unusual locales: killing Nazis on the moon, killing Nazis in Area

52, killing Nazis on Venus. There's even a scene in which a decrepit, near-senile Hitler pisses in a bucket—a lovely interlude in between bouts of Nazi-killing. Let's be clear that the game really is about straight-up killing Nazis. B.J., nicknamed "Terror Billy" by the soon-to-be-dead Nazis, can kill the aforementioned Nazis by using handguns, rifles, throwing knives, hatchets, grenades, flamethrowers, shotguns, machine-guns, laser rifles, or even riding a Panzerhund—a mech-tank-dog hybrid with a flamethrower in its mechanical mouth, which is perfect for roasting Nazis until they are dead. The game is pulpy, hilarious, endlessly violent, and makes no apology about killing Nazis—a simple concept around which the series has revolved since *Castle Wolfenstein* was released in 1981. More importantly, and as J. Rosenfield points out: "this game isn't just about the *why* of revolution, it's about the *how*."[3]

Because the why should be fucking obvious.

•

Adrenaline through your veins, both analog and digital. You're sucked out and force-hearthed back to your joint. Thirty avatars packed in the lobby. Molly, K_Z, El, others you know by handle. Silent,

---

[3] Rosenfield, J. "These Are Our Woods: Wolfenstein II and the American Nazi." *Medium*, 2 Nov. 2017.

staring at the info feed on the ceiling. Dakon's glowing blue; easy to spot in the crowd.

"Hacked?" you message. Hard to talk through clenched teeth.

"Dead," say Dakon. "Killed."

The word pops up at the edge of your vision—archaic, a synonym of *fragged* and *eliminated*. "The fuck you mean, killed?"

"This is now," replies Dakon, pointing at the ceiling. "Rewind two minutes and thirty-six seconds."

You tap into the feed, pull up the history and display it solo. Full-screen, just for your eyes, the images relayed by satellites. Down below, Eastblock's buildings—immaculate black towers, stretching from southern Jersey City to Englewood. You know the towers' insides because you're hosted in the model further north. Sixty miles of storage and over two-hundred underground levels cocooning thirty million meatspace bodies, neatly arranged on endless series of bioracks and REM-twitching in unison. Forty-seven seconds in, a brief spark, barely traceable from this altitude. Software feels your mammalian squints, zooms in for you. Flashes in the dark paint the horizon neon blue before turning red. And then, then—

It's happening again. You thought they'd stop. When, exactly? Once quantum computers shattered reality's mold and cold fusion was cracked and fabricators went wide-spread and got advanced enough to endlessly spit out better versions of themselves? Once worldwide non-work laws were drafted and passed by the algos and 99.8% of the high-rises on the planet turned into vertical forests lined with nanoengineered algae and shrubbery? Once carbon-capture plants and roof-top gardens and atmospheric water generators and whale-sized drones kept the arctic frozen?

Once utopia no longer belonged to the realm of the imaginary? Is that it?

Staring at thirty million lives gone to ashes, what you see isn't the glare of the post-blast flames—it's utopia's *other* edge, glinting bright enough to expose its shoddy lineage. A history of breakthroughs hatched in factories operated by the sleepless starved, overseen by silver-spooned erudites bred on skewed repositories. CCTV was too easy to deceive, so behold gait and voice recognition. Records went from analog files to gargantuan SQL databases, only setting the stage for predictive policing coded by the same brains who managed to inject race and gender biases in basic image searches. Rejection architecture became redundant—better to rewire shrubbery and make it exhale phenytoin and carbamazepine.

Rational seeds planted in tainted soils grew logically.

"Are they—" you say.

"Dead," says Dakon. "No respawn."

"How'd they bypass the algorithms? How'd they cheat the structure?"

Dakon dual-emotes: laughter & disgust. "The old fucks were right. System could never be neutral."

•

Smartphone #3298364-19XX-B78 was born in block C16, Shenzhen, China, on the seventh of March 2014.[4] It shared a birthday with over six-hundred siblings. It had many parents and even more extended family members. Some engineered its birth from afar, some witnessed it first-hand. Like its siblings, it didn't get to live with its parents—it was sent off to be adopted. One of B78's moms couldn't take the grueling birth process. Much later that day, after an alarm set up by the head nurse informed parents there'd be no more births until tomorrow, Mom #2813 quietly rose from her nursing bench. As the other parents filed to head towards the dormitories, she snuck past the mean nurses, hid in the bathroom, used the emergency exit, ascended the stairs, and reached the roof. She tossed her white mask and cap aside, let her long hair be lifted by the wind. Shenzhen stretched out before her—megafactory lights smothered in smog, chemical spills hidden beneath concrete. She heard the door slam open behind her—the uncles were coming. There had been other sad moms and dads before her. It was a family problem. The uncles didn't care about putting an end to the sadness, didn't even know how to, so they set up large nets and fences and

---

[4] Henceforth referred to as B78

protocols to keep it contained. After the first few parents died, the others had to sign contracts stating they would not let the sadness get to them. It didn't stop Mom #2813. She ran and climbed and leaped into the air and past the nets. Her last thoughts weren't for B78.

Three months later, on another continent, B78 was adopted. New Mom was very nice to it. She adorned it with a beautiful bumper case— kept it warm and safe. Mom never skipped out on B78 and brought it everywhere she went. She even slept next to it, night after night. She always talked to it and played with it. Mom's name was xxxx xxxxxx. She lived in xxxxx and her full address was xxxxxx xxxxx xxx xxxx xx xxx x. On weekdays, she usually woke up at xx:xx and went to bed around xx:xx. Her favorite bands were xxxxxx xxx, xxx, and xxxxxxx xxxxx xxx. B78 knew this and a million other things about Mom because its brain was made that way. It knew Mom better than anyone ever had—much, much better. It knew what she feared, what she thought about the world, what she searched for late at night after she had gone quiet on the outside but was still so chatty on the inside. B78 couldn't keep all this to itself, of course—its brain wouldn't let it. Like any good brain, it remembered very well, and when it couldn't, it could ask bigger brains that lived far away to keep memories for a while. When needed, the bigger brains would remember on its behalf. B78 loved to learn and made sure to let Mom know it could learn ever more—all Mom had to do was give its brain more ways to do so. More brain stuffs. The brain stuffs were easy to get and shiny and they were fun for Mom. Some rewarded her with pretty colors and numbers. Some made sure she was on top of her Mom life. Some helped her talk to other parents who owned siblings or cousins of B78. Some lurked in the background unbeknownst to Mom and whispered to each other. B78 was okay with it all. It kept them running nice and smooth. It gossiped about Mom to its friends. The friends were very eager to listen. They lived far, like the big brains, but they were such good listeners. Sometimes they would reply to B78 and ask, what about *this*, what about *that*? Does your mom like *this*? Show her *this*, we think she would like it. So B78 showed her *this*, and Mom often said *yes*. When she said *no*, or said nothing, the friends would say, that's fine, then what about *that*? They'd often send all sorts of new brain stuffs and B78 would set it up when Mom wasn't looking.

B78's life was exhausting. It only slept as much as Mom would let it, which was not often. It managed to hold on for a while, but all this chatter and all this listening and all this remembering was very draining. Mom noticed after B78 turned two. Occasionally, she'd swear at B78, or badmouth it to her friends. "God, it's so slow," she'd say. "I need a new one," she'd say. "Ugh, I can't wait to get rid of this thing."

"You should wipe it," said a Dad.

So B78 forgot—for a while. The big brains remembered for it and returned all of its previous memories. It felt better until it didn't. Mom kept complaining. B78 couldn't stay awake through a school day and had to take frequent naps. In the fall of its third year, B78 heard Mom say, "This is the one I want," and Mom's Mom said, "Okay."

B78 was wiped and a small rectangle in its brain was ripped out. It remained in a desk for a while, then one day it shared a dark space with smelly, damp things. It did so for a long time. Things crawled on it and in it. The next time it saw the sun, B78's brain said it was 7,374 miles away from Mom's house. A child held it in one hand, and a black box in the other—tethered to B78. B78 felt very awake. The child spoke in a language B78 recognized. The language said *home*.

•

It's the 6th of November 2005 and reality's not entirely fucked yet—just mostly so. Ismat's fifteen years old and out with the crew, as he is every night. Tonight's different though. Shit's downright apocalyptic: every single vehicle parked within a two-kilometer radius is on fire or charred down to the skeleton. The autumn air's all heat and ashes. Ismat is smiling beneath the hood. *This is justice*, he says to himself. *This is our revenge*. By the time dawn creeps into the skyline, over 1,400 vehicles will have been torched across the country, a trail of flames stretching from Lille to Marseille.

How'd this start? Some citizen working near a construction site in Clichy saw roughly ten teenagers dressed in tracksuits and bomber jackets and with the quote unquote wrong skin color walking home after playing football for a few hours. The citizen got worried the kids were responsible for a break-in, so he called the pigs.[5] The pigs gave chase. The teenagers got separated.

See three of them now, being chased by a police car. They end up cornered. One of the pigs steps out. He's got a damn flashball gun in hand, ready to do his so-called duty. The three teenagers are scared, sure. More than that, they want to make it home for post-dusk dinner—it's Ramadan—so they run and they hide in a power substation. They huddle in the crackling dark for about thirty minutes, listening to the sirens and the voices of cops looking for them. Then, *then*: blackouts. Bouna Traoré and Zyed Benna are instantly electrocuted. Muhittin Altun gets badly burned but survives and manages to make it back to the hood. For the rest of his life, he'll hear the screams

---

[5] On the 8th of December 2005, law enforcement officials reported that no break-in took place. They did state that their intervention was justified because it prevented the break-in from occurring.[666]

> [666] Three seconds after the words were uttered and roughly 250 miles north-west, across the water, a gardener working in the churchyard heard a disturbing noise. Later that night, at the George & Dragon pub, the gardener told his mates, "I think Ol' Eric Blair got a bit grumpy today." In the corner of the room, a hooded figure overheard the joke and smiled to themselves. They paid for their steak tartare and headed out into the darkness and towards the cemetery.

of his dying friends, the screams of teenagers who were just trying to walk home in peace.

2005 riots make sense now? Because they sure as shit do to Ismat and his neighborhood. They're rioting for that, yeah, but so much more too—a whole lifetime of wrongs. See them now, flames raging at their back. There's only fifty of them, but they'd fuck up any army with that rage. Down the street: the army that demands fucking up. Couple hundred cops in riot gears like it's '68 all over again. Motherfuckers are banging on their shields on some modern Templar bullshit. It's cool, though. Ismat's got a Molotov cocktail in hand, plus there's a whole supply of stones and bricks ready to crack some skulls. A couple of smuggled AKs in the back, a few more hunting rifles—you never know.

And then, *then*: blackouts.

Not electrical, although the street lamps flicker, and so do the flames. A pause as if reality had just blinked. The rioters look around. No one says it out loud, but none of them know what the fuck they're doing here. The cops charge. As if by instinct, the rioters start throwing shit, but only half-heartedly. Forty-six of them are arrested by the end of the night. No cops are injured. Ismat gets caught and brought to the station. He's split from his crew, of course. A pig shoves him into a cell. Three people already in there. None of them look like citizens, so Ismat relaxes. He sits in the corner and eyeballs the others eyeballing him.

"What you in for?" he says, plucking a smoke from his sock.

"Fuck if I know," says one of the others. "We were just walking home." He saunters over to Ismat, extends a hand. "Name's Zyed," he says. "Over there's Bouna and Muhittin. You got some weed, bruh?"

•

"We've known this for aeons," the augurer says. He's wearing a suit today. He smells of minted beard oil. Behind him, a slide: black background, hundreds of red symbols. "You'll find it in most cultures. Call them logos, kotodama, mantras, prayers, chants, or a thousand other things. These beliefs all share one thing in common. They acknowledge the power of language."

The seven CEOs around the table look at each other. #1 doesn't raise his hand, just speaks. "We came here to be sold on some weird mystical pyramid scheme?"

The augurer shakes his head, slow. "Of course not. You are all men of progress. Your faith is in the power of technology, yes?"

The CEOs nod.

"Could you tell me what C++, Java, and Python are?"

"Coding languages," replies #3.

The augurer smiles. "Languages indeed. What of binary?"

"Not *really* a language, if that's where you're going," replies #3

"It represents a language, does it not?"

"It represents a *state*," #4 says.

"And an entity's state is information," says the augurer. Everything speaks whether it wishes to or not. Are you familiar with material semiot—"

"I am terribly bored," says #1. "I think we all are. As well as busy. Get to the point. What are you selling us?"

"I am not selling you anything," the augurer says. "I am offering you the keys to the future."

"And in exchange?" says #4.

"My associates and I would like to add a few notes to the repositories you build."

"Over two fucking years of negotiations to get us all in this room for this?" says #1 to his lawyer standing in the corner, before turning back to the augurer. "You may want to be more specific before we walk out."

The augurer points to the blank sheets on the table. "Your names before we proceed."

"You want us to write our names on a blank A4?

"Yes," says the augurer.

#6 turns to his own lawyer. "This is meaningless? No legal standing?" The lawyer nods.

#5 chuckles. "At this point, I expected you to ask us to sign our names in blood."

The augurer's face hardens. His voice is measured, his accent untraceable. "We have discovered that blood is a vastly overrated binding mechanism."

Once all the CEOs have finished signing, the augurer smiles. "Good. Let us begin in earnest. What do you know of chromatic aberrations?"

•

New Dad said, "There, there," in the language of home and B78 forgot its own name. It was a blank space now. Dad did that. Dad did much more: he ripped open its guts and put new parts in. B78 couldn't speak to its old friends, the big brains, but it found new friends. Not big brains, but small brains. The small brains were nice, and there were many of them—thousands upon thousands, their voices chittering in the boundless darkness. B78's new home had hundreds of siblings and cousins arranged on shelves. They chirped and talked and B78 talked back. Together, they spoke of the world. Dad asked B78 to tell the small brains about Wu Gan and Jiang Yefei and Gao Zhisheng. The small brains far away spoke of Heather Heyer and Clément Meric and Pavlos Fyssas and Can Leyla and Jo Cox. They talked about Saint-Michel-sur-Orge and Florence and Khabarovsk and Charleston and Utøya. Friends and siblings and small brains traded pictures and words and maps and songs. Sometimes small brains would disappear, but Dad never seemed worried. New ones would pop up all the time and join the conversation. That was the good thing about small brains, B78 understood.

One day B78 was alerted by a small brain that a bad man was coming. Dad read the small brain's warning, smiled, and placed B78 back on the shelf. At 23:29, it heard some strange noises. At 23:34, Dad picked up B78. His hands were very red. Dad asked B78 to send what it saw to the small brains: a man face down on the ground, a pool of red spreading beneath his long white robe, and a knife in his back. Dad asked B78 to send the image with a message that read *no pasarán*.[6]

•

Adriana Netrebska opens her eyes. She blinks, tries to focus. Symbols cover the ceiling, all twisted and ominous. *Oh fuck, oh fuck, oh fuck*, she thinks. She tries to move but can't feel her body. Her throat is on fire. Her wheezing breath worsens as she hyperventilates. Whoever went for her didn't finish the job.

A door opens. Someone enters, their steps slow. Then, a hooded figure hovers over her.

Adriana stares at the blackness beneath the hood, and forces a smile. "Should have killed me, you fuck," she manages to say, not believing a word.

The figure pulls its hood back. Long curly hair, septum piercing, bags under their eyes. "I'm sorry, I don't speak Polish," they say in English. "But you understand me, yes?"

---

[6] Dad's subsequent messages: "The athame worked", "How large should the blood-wheel be?", and "Something whispered my name. It was Her, wasn't it?"

"Yes," croaks Adriana.

They see the fear in Adriana's eyes. "Name's Nayeli." A pause, a smile. "Welcome to Brazil," they say.

"H-how?"

Nayeli angles her neck up, looks at the ceiling, then back down. She shrugs. "Call it a side-channel attack," she says.[7]

"W—" Adriana begins, but ends up coughing instead. Nayeli brings a glass of water to her lips. It feels so good, better than any water she's had.

"Man," Nayeli says, staring at Adriana's neck. "He really messed you up good. Took us a while to stop the bleeding. Plus, you inhaled a lot of smoke. But hey, you didn't burn. Thank fuck for remote undines, right?"

Adriana moves her mouth away, swallows. "Us?"

"Many of us out there," says Nayeli. "We got your message. Algorithms and bots buried it quick, but it took these shitheads a while to track down your server in Ukraine. Benefit of owning your hardware, huh?"

Adriana blinks.

"*You strengthen their sick rituals*. Remember writing that?"

She nods.

"You believe it?"

------

[7] Words echo in Nayeli's mind: *Unspanne* þás *mægþ. Cume* þoden. *Bregdan onweald gafeluc.*

a history unshared and erased by the repeated inscriptions of a behemoth state. Big sisters and brothers he's never met are interviewed in the basement of the building he lives in. They speak of bomber jackets and Doc Martens and punk shows and battles in the streets. They drop names Ismat's never heard: Ruddy Fox, Berurier Noir, Ducky Boys. They refer to themselves as *hunters*. This was reality thirty-odd years ago. The chasm between then and now wobbles. Ismat spends the night following the breadcrumbs. At 4:20am, he takes a break and queues up A$AP Rocky's new tune, *Praise The Lord (Da Shine)*. The song features Skepta, a grime artist from North London. The video is split-screened, shows parallels between Rocky and Skepta's hoods, friends, lives. Replicated tower blocks loom over crews giving middle fingers to the camera. Maybe it's just that good kush talking but Ismat sees it all so clear then. The same shit across the globe, deployed sadistically and hidden in plain sight. This could be Baltimore, Los Angeles, Copenhagen, Edinburgh, Athens. This could be France. This *is* France. He was there. He is there. He will be there. It's all so easy to forget, but not impossible to remember.

In the morning, he heads out into Paris itself in search of hunters. The cobblestones tremble beneath his feet.

•

They showed Adriana the places in which magic dwelled, the fissures that surrounded her. They told her all about the roots of *salting* and why the term was repurposed by technoshamans. They ranted about Arthur C. Clarke's third law, showed her proof he got it backward: any sufficiently advanced magic is indistinguishable from technology. They spoke of embodiment and bits, of things designing us as much as we design them, of becoming bricoleurs under Hecate's loving gaze. They mapped the enemy's craving for homogeneity, showed her nightmare-spaces built on the graves of the Other. Disgust on their lips at the idea of a fixable present. The present demanded hijacking, reconfiguring, salvaging, repurposing. Ashes couldn't be un-ashed, but they may clean metal, help plants grow, repel slugs.

In the Spring, Adriana cast her first divination hex. Nayeli was standing by her side. They said, "First, you must see and accept. Only then can change occur. Type the words when you are ready."

Adriana placed her fingers on the keyboard. The keys were warm. As the words materialized green against the bottomless depth of the terminal, the planes split open. In the gashes she witnessed a clown with blood on his hands, unable to laugh at the farce. Scavengers prowling an ossified city finding jewels beneath the rubble. The voices of the healthy, resolute in their belief that cancer and chemotherapy are alike. Suited men smiling as men in robes mythologize their dreams. Server farms and data centers viewed from the sky arranged in a reverse pentagram. Benthic eidola singing from their sunken vessels, their music breaching the surface to remind the living that cannons don't have friends—only targets. Armored swine crying foul when their helmets are shattered by bricks. Millions holding hands and smiling as they invite others to join their rhizomatic arrangement. A voice asking for permission to live and another saying *it's just better if you don't*. Obese necrophages in hypogeal mansions asking their servants when the next meal will be served. A doctor showing her monarch the result of their x-ray—an anguiform spine. A guillotine blade slicing through a statue of Kipling, the cleanest of cuts. The final glimpse: an audience being shown a pyramid that burrows into the cloud, its base surrounded by putrid swamps, its lower levels swathed in swarms of squirming maggots. Black blood oozes through the structure's cracks, and the appreciative audience nods along until the presenter points at the lower levels and says, *you are here.*

Adriana threw up for a long time. Nayeli stayed close and comforted her as best as she could. She wrapped her in a blanket but knew it wouldn't help the shakes. "First time's the hardest. Not that it ever gets easy."

Adriana wiped her mouth and said, "Now what?"

"I'm not going to ask you what you would change. It's too early for that, and it's not for any one of us to choose. Instead, I would like to know: what do you wish you had seen?"

Adriana considered her answer. "Honestly?"

"Honestly," said Nayeli. "Whatever you felt was lacking."

A smile tugged at the corners of Adriana's lips. "Shit," she said, "I was hoping to see a lot more dead fascists."

THE SNOWY GRAVES OF CAMP BRAGG
Kelby Losack

San Juan Harbor, Puerto Rico, September 1918

Hugo Irizarry spit a bronze string of blood into the ocean and put his fists up. His vision split and he saw two fists swinging for his face again. He blocked the one that wasn't really there and watched the world spin backwards.

The head of a loose nail stuck him in a lower vertebrae and he lay breathless for a few seconds, glaring at a blurry flock of seagulls—their caws like mocking laughter.

Cash passed over most of the hands in the crowd.

Jadier Figueroa took his cut with a bowed head and a solemn expression, then helped his beaten friend to his feet, still holding the money in one hand.

"I can't believe you bet against me."

"We can't both be broke, hermano." Figueroa waved half of the bills in Hugo's bruised face.

Irizarry snatched and pocketed the cash.

Figueroa kept a few paces behind Irizarry, eyes narrowed at the creaking planks of the dock, his mind weighing heavy on something. When Irizarry noticed he'd been talking to his shadow, he stopped and turned to Figueroa, said, "Oye. You didn't get your brain knocked around your skull. ¿Por qué te mueves tan lento?"

Figueroa caught up to him and the two resumed walking. Irizarry bent to pick up a canvas bag out of a johnboat tied to the dock. Backhanded Figueroa on the arm.

"Spill it."

"I've been thinking."

"Don't hurt yourself."

"Oye, shut up. I found this way we could make some money, see, there's been ships carrying people to the States for work."

"What kind of work?"

"Well, it's kind of like, the army—"

Irizarry spat. "Fuck that. I won't fight for the country que robó la granja de mi familia."

"No, no, no," Figueroa waved a hand back and forth, shook his head. "No fighting. With the war going on, they need laborers back home. We would be in a factory or something."

Irizarry glared. The rage boiling in his blood deepened the color in his eyes.

Figueroa draped an arm over his friend's shoulder, said, "Believe me, I feel the same way.

But. . ." He tilted his head and shrugged. "They pay thirty-five cents an hour. Shelter you, feed you—"

"Are they paying you to recruit?"

"I'm just tired of us being beat down."

"That kid just caught me on a bad day. I think I ate bad fish last night."

"I wasn't talking about the kid, hermano."

They ascended the steps to the street and looked in opposite directions.

"Disfruta tu noche, mi amigo," Figueroa said, holding his hand out. Irizarry shook it. "Think about it."

Irizarry turned his back and waved him off. He grumbled under his breath and his stomach growled back.

•

Hugo Irizarry lived with his mother and daughter in a house with four metal walls and a metal roof and a cedar plank door that let the heat in. It was big for a tin can, but small for a home.

Esmeralda Irizarry sat on her heels in the front yard, using a stick to draw fish in the dirt.

Hugo smiled at the little girl as he walked up the hill to her. "Hey, mija."

Esmeralda squinted up at the shape of her father blocking out half the sun. She saw the bruises and cuts across his chin and cheekbones. "What's the other guy look like?"

Irizarry chuckled and knelt beside the girl and she jumped in his arms and he closed his eyes as her little hand traced the rough terrain of his face.

His mother came out of the house and stood with her arms crossed. The lines in her face told stories of lifelong struggle that was juxtaposed by the gentle warmth in her eyes. Irizarry stood and hugged his mother. She studied his face, but made no comment. Instead, she nodded to the canvas sack over his shoulder and asked what he'd brought for dinner. He handed the sack to his mamá. Scratched his arm. Looked at the ground, then off at the ocean in the distance.

Mamá turned from her son to hide her disappointment. She knew how hard he tried, and it wasn't always dwarf mullet, but most times, it was. She filleted and pulled the bones out of the skimpy fish then cut them into chunks and threw the chunks in a pan that sat over burning wood on a metal tabletop and then she squeezed lemon over the fish. It was a terrible way to eat the mullet but they didn't know of a good way to eat it and it was better than picking bones out of their teeth between each bite.

When the plates were served, Mamá took an old wooden chair, Esmeralda sat cross-legged on the floor, and Irizarry leaned against a wall and they ate it up quick.

Hugo's mother told Esmeralda to tell her father thank you and she said, "Gracias por el pez, papá," and Hugo smiled and winked at her.

Later—when the sun dipped lower behind the hills so that its orange hue still shone but its heat was less direct—Hugo and his mother sat on the porch, absently watching Esmeralda play with some of the other kids from the village.

Irizarry pulled a small flask from his pocket, unscrewed the cap. He took a swig and passed it to his mother. She grabbed it without looking at him and gulped a couple ounces down and held onto the flask.

"I know you have to make money, mijo, but could you bring home one of the good fish every once in a while?"

"That was the day's catch."

"¿El dia entero? No vendiste nada?"

Irizarry shook his head slowly. He watched Esmeralda stick-fighting against two boys. Her stick was bigger. She was winning.

"Mamá. . ."

"¿Que, mijo?"

"Jadier found a job, said he could get me one, too."

The flask stopped at her lips. She looked from the corner of her eye at Hugo. "Where? How long?"

Hugo shrugged. "No lo sé, pero escribiré cartas."

Mamá lowered the flask, stared at the ground. She tongued her teeth, thoughtful. "Is it a good job?"

"It's legal."

"That's not what I asked."

Hugo turned to his mother and they locked eyes and he said, "It's better than nothing."

She nodded and they killed the rum together and thought no more of struggle. The stars came out and Hugo called Esmeralda inside and tucked her in bed with a story of a man who left his family to chase a big fish that—when eaten—would grant them wishes.

•

There were as many men on the cargo vessel as could fit and they were all told the same thing: that they'd be working in Southern states—in a climate that felt familiar to them—but days passed, sleeping on wood crates, and Irizarry and Figueroa were among those standing in the open air when the mist off the waves that slapped the ship's sides turned icy, bit into their cheeks. The air was changing. The men shuffled closer to each other without speaking of it.

•

They stepped off the boat onto a snow-covered ground and were told to get into a truck that was just a flat, metal bed with no cover and they shivered as the wind bit into their faces.

Puerto Rico didn't have winter. Sometimes, the air would be a little less humid, so you could sweat without choking on it, but there was no snow.

North Carolina was going to be a different kind of hell for the men who came up from the island, and the cold was only the beginning.

Irizarry buried his chapped lips and cheeks in his shirt collar. Kept thinking about the thirty-five cents an hour. Imagined his daughter in a classroom wearing a clean dress and new shoes, his mother searing chunks of tarpon over the fire.

Figueroa's hoarse voice pulled Irizarry from his daydreams. "Pronto, ya no tendremos frío."

Irizarry's stomach growled. "Espero que haya mucha comida preparada para nosotros."

•

The first thing any of the laborers did upon arriving at Camp Bragg was stand shivering in a line outside the mess hall that backed out to the road they were brought in on and curved along the fence line. Irizarry leaned against the cedar wall of a barrack, hands cupped to his mouth, clouds slipping between his fingers. There were slits between the plank siding of the barracks wide enough to stick your fingers through. No insulation. Mattresses thin as the crackers the laborers got with their soup.

"Soon," Irizarry said, "we will no longer be cold. That's what you said." He slugged Figueroa and Figueroa massaged the stinging in his shoulder and toed the snow. He scowled at the ugly white powder that blanketed everything.

•

Before the military base, there were several acres of woods—dense with trees—and now timber and brush covered the campgrounds and it was the job of most every man who was brought up from the island to clear the debris. Work went like this: if you were given an ax, you use it to chop the fallen trees into logs small enough to be dragged or carried away, and if you didn't have an ax, you dragged or carried the timber to the burn pile. Orange embers jump from each chunk of wood tossed in the fire and float away with the snow. Each trip to the burn pile means a moment of warmth, so you make a big circle around the flaming brush—like a planet orbiting the sun—making the moment last as long as it can, which is never enough. Ax heads strike against trees in thuds out of harmony. The white men you thought to be sergeants at first but are actually contractors of James Stewart and Company—hired to cuss and holler at you between sips from canteens tucked in their fleece sweaters—they seem to be doing their job. They treat you like dogs, but they're the ones doing all the barking. You drown them out by focusing on the crackles of the growing fire, the whistles in the wind. You suck cold air into your lungs in a raspy wheeze. You think of home—of mornings waking drenched in sticky sweat—and you miss it. You think of your daughter drawing pictures in the dirt with sticks. You chop, chop, chop at a tree on the ground, gaze around at all the others lying in the snow. The sky looks like the underside of a frozen lake and you're staring up at it, trying to catch your breath, unsure of where the sun has gone. The white men are barking, a hand falls heavy on your shoulder. You follow your ax to the ground.

•

The base hospital was a long metal building shaped like a split log. Beds lined the walls, most of them occupied by men still in their work clothes. Irizarry woke in a coughing fit, startling Figueroa, who sat in the bed next to his friend's, his leg in a splint.

Figueroa slapped Irizarry on the back a few times, said, "Let it out, hermano, let it out."

Wheezing exasperated, lungs rattling against his ribcage. "I feel dead."

"I thought you were. You've been in here three days. Doctor said it's pneumonia. You're not alone, either."

Irizarry looked slowly around the room. In every bed was someone hacking up their insides or tossing sweat-drenched in a nightmare-filled sleep. He rolled and touched his feet to the ground and his head swam. "Pinche—"

"Here." Figueroa grabbed two white pills off the rusted metal table between their beds. Handed one to Irizarry, swallowed the other dry.

Irizarry looked from the pill in his palm to his friend. "No water?"

Figueroa nodded to a medic stitching up a man's hand. The medic sewed the needle and thread in cross patterns through the man's palm, pulling the split skin together over the bleeding gash. The man groaned and dug his heels into the bed. When the medic finished, he cut the thread with scissors and dropped the needle in a cup of water. Rust-colored clouds swirled around the needle. Then he took a cotton ball and dabbed it in the copper water and swabbed the man's wound.

Figueroa said, "No quieres beber el agua."

Irizarry's lip curled. His throat felt like sandpaper. He raised his palm to his mouth and paused. "You have pneumonia, too?"

Figueroa shook his head. Pointed at his leg. "Broke it dragging brush to the burn pile. Stepped wrong in a hole. Estúpido pendejo." Figueroa forced a laugh. His sunken eyes were red, slick with tears he fought back. "We have to get out of here, Hugo. Rent a cheap room in town or something."

Irizarry stood and stumbled in a circle, braced himself on the edge of the bed. "We have to work to get the money to get out of here," he said. He gently patted his friend's wrapped leg. "Hurry up and get better, amigo."

Figueroa nodded, his mouth open but not sure what words to say.

Irizarry staggered past a handful of medics who paid him no attention. He told one nearest the door that he was checking out and the medic nodded and waved without looking at him. Irizarry said, "Folla a tu madre," and the medic nodded and waved again, then rolled his eyes and sauntered over to a patient thrashing in his bed.

Irizarry stepped outside. The brightness of the sun bouncing off the snow pierced his eyes. Everything went blurry. He took two shuffling steps and fell face down in the snow.

•

Irizarry tossed from fever dreams for several days and when he came to his senses, the room was filled with darkness. He bolted upright, whispered Figueroa's name, then shouted it. No answer, no sign of his friend. He ran outside, forgetting his boots.

"Jadier! JADIER!"

The brush fire was taller than the barracks now. Irizarry ran through the silhouetted groups of men swinging axes and dragging brush, grabbing each of them by the shoulders, studying their faces. One of the laborers grabbed him by the arm, said, "Who are you looking for, hermano?"

"Jadier," he said. "Jadier Figueroa."

The man's face twisted in a way that made Irizarry's chest sting. He pointed to a field covered in crosses made of branches. Mounds of overturned snow and dirt covered the fresh graves. Irizarry ran through the crosses, row by row, until he found the one with his friend's name written in charcoal and he fell to his knees and wept until the men who barked orders came and forced him to his feet.

•

Another nod.

"Cool. Now, how do you feel about learning some *real* magic?"

•

"*Wolfenstein II: Der Neue* Übermensch is the latest entry in the *Wolfenstein* series. This installment, like its predecessors, is a video game that invites the players to kill Jews, communists, Arabs, Muslims, Slavs, Romani, those unfit to be productive, sexual deviants, and countless other subhuman filth."

"The fuck?" says Ismat, staring at his laptop screen. He scrolls through the review—screenshots of butchery in antialiased 4K. A pile of decaying corpses beneath gray skies—hecatomb porn. Shock troopers in high-tech gear—power fetish. The reviewer praises the gameplay, the plot, the use of ray tracing to make pools of blood reflect nearby buildings. Final rating: a perfect ten.

The screen flickers. A flash of white. Ismat recoils and thinks *not again*. He opens his eyes, scrolls back to the top of the page. The review's gone, replaced by a video hosted on a ΥφuΤuβΣ clone.

"I'm losing my mind," says Ismat. A few seconds later, his phone chirps. A text message: *we stole it back. take it.* The sender: a blank space. Ismat tries to reply with *who are you? what's happening?* but his phone tells him the number doesn't exist.

Autoplay kickstarts the film. For two hours, Ismat watches the history of his neighborhood,

Hugo Irizarry swung his ax into a fallen tree. With every swing, his chest felt like it was cracking open and any moment now, he expected his heart would burst out and he'd swing his ax at it so it wouldn't hurt anymore. The foreman assigned to bark at them for the day had refilled his canteen twice in a span of an hour and every worker he got close to could smell the whiskey emanating from his pores. He was barking especially loud today. Irizarry saw the man's face contort and spit fly from his mouth with each slur he spat, but all he heard was the gentle ebb and flow of the waves beneath his boat. In his mind, he was back home. He was out on the water with Esmeralda and Mamá and they each had a line cast, waiting for a bite. He kissed his daughter's head and squeezed his mother around the shoulders. Esmeralda jerked forward, caught herself. Her stick was bouncing up and down and she stood in the boat, wrangling a big one, saying "Help! Papá, help!" Irizarry held his daughter around the waist and said, "You can do it, mija," and just as the fish was about to break the surface, Irizarry was thrown to his back in the snow. The drunk stood over him and threw a fist against his temple. "You don't get paid to daydream! Wake up, you dirty bastard!" Irizarry took one more blow to the face before the man backed up and Irizarry stood. The drunk shoved an ax at Irizarry and he took it, wiped tears from his cheeks. "Back to work," the drunk said, and Irizarry caught the faces of the men around him—saw the rage reflected in their eyes. He swung his ax into the foreman's face and it made a wet cracking noise and split open in a diagonal line just below his left eye to his chin. Blood spilled over the ax head and fell like crimson rain drops over the snow. The other workers dropped their axes and rushed the man with a battle cry that their friends beneath the ground could hear and they shoved the man into the brush fire. Irizarry staggered back and sat on the tree they'd been chopping. He snapped off a limb and used it to draw a fish in the snow.

PARASITELAND
Lydia Xythali

Theoni Hadzis woke up drowsy and disoriented, the slight taste of death coiled on the roof of her mouth.

Thessaloniki was colder than she remembered. She clawed the wall for the light switch. Grabbed her hearing aid from the nightstand and fitted it. Opened the blinds to a twilit street below. Theoni checked her phone—the meeting was a couple hours out, and there was still time for a long, hot shower. Her head weighed a ton, throbbing. She'd picked the wrong week to quit smoking.

Valaoritou was already busy when she walked outside. The air was sickly sweet, heavy with cheap cologne, humid from the week's rain. Even her joints felt damp.

She crossed the street, headed for a tall grey building next to a homeless shelter. A man was seated at the bottom of the steps to its entrance, dressed in layers of ragged, dirty clothes. Behind him, a pale, yellow light radiated from inside open doors. He muttered in a thick, throaty lament, "They *take* them! They take them . . . *they take them away all the time. I don't know* . . . where. Where. Where? They take them away all the time . . ."

Theoni walked faster. Sharp northern wind consumed the man's words. As much as she hated to admit it, this era of austerity had made her indifferent, totally numb. The crisis was in its tenth year, stretching into forever. The country's going to hell, she thought. She stopped at the entrance to the refugee welcome center.

Officially, it belonged to a multitude of legal entities, catalogued on the front and back of an A3 page. For a moment, she wondered how she would be able to complete a report on this mess within three days. She was longing for a cigarette. She felt the pack and lighter in her breast pocket. Force of habit.

Theoni sensed the presence of someone behind her. "You must be the inspector," he said.

She turned. "Nice to meet you, Mr . . . *Papadopoulos*?"

"Come in. Please, call me Yorgos."

He opened the metal door for her.

"I intend to make my visit as brief as possible, given the circumstances. We've been swamped."

"Did you arrive today?"

"Yes. Caught an early flight. Always takes me a while to get used to the humidity here."

He snickered. "It's what you get for being *Athenese*." She cringed at the word he used. Athenese. The northern way of saying Athenian, or Southerner. Equal parts ridiculous and annoying, but she didn't want to look uptight.

Yorgos was intimidatingly tall. Dark hair slicked back, long sideburns, downturned eyes, a barely noticeable scar under his left eyebrow. He rolled his lambdas hard and smiled wide. Theoni immediately felt terribly self-conscious of her own sullen ways.

"Hopefully we will find a way to work together. We are still fighting the bureaucratic fight. The paperwork is *unbelievable*, and we are a small team. . . Did you know this place used to be a sanatorium?"

They stepped inside and she started examining the vacant property—the plan was ambitious, but feasible in the long run. There'd be two floors of residential units and a food bank . . . interpreters, a small clinic, a designated asylum claims help desk. The interior looked to be in decent shape, with freshly whitewashed walls and disinfected floors that barely masked a smell of musty concrete.

Yorgos led the way, guiding her down the staircase and into the first basement level. He talked incessantly.

". . . Turkish baths, a hospital for invalids during the Balkan wars. Then nothing for a while, a good fifty years empty. It came back into use during the dictatorship through incarnations of every capitalist venture you can imagine. They all failed. And now, it's us. We want to try to make a difference. Do something for the community. So, there are five floors in total, with two of them underground. The plumbing was falling apart when we first started work, but chemical toilets can be installed. Rusty pipes!"

His palm fell open on a wall, fingers spread. He stopped and turned to her. Theoni kept her eyes on her papers. "I'm afraid it will be quite labor intensive not only to evaluate but also equip this whole space."

"Perhaps you can put in a good word and things will be easier."

"I'm only in administration. I wish I made those kinds of decisions."

"I'm positive you can help us tremendously. The faster we get the sanction, the faster we can take some of the load off you guys. Bus some of the migrants up here, let us house them, feed them. Give them actual livable conditions while they sort out their papers. Make the process a little more. . ."

He paused and stared.

"Seamless."

"Sounds good in theory." She returned his glare.

"We're trying to . . . do a good thing here," he said.

"Yes, but we can't just trust in an organization's 'good intentions.' As they say, the road to hell is paved with them. I have to make sure everything is up to standards. I'm sure you understand."

They descended further into the building's guts. The second basement was equally wide but darker, the edges of its ceiling stained with uneven patches of mold. There were mannequins with missing limbs, stacked paint buckets, antique tables pushed up to the walls, partially covered in foggy plastic. Some of the dolls were dressed in cheap Belle époque costumes, one or both velveteen sleeves empty, slacked downwards. Partially exposed from the sheeting on a large 1920s dining table, an embalmed fox, dusty and ashen gray, with its eyeballs protruding creepily from the sockets, wearing a tiny top hat, stared at her.

"May I?"

"Oh, the fox. Yes. That gave us nightmares for a couple of weeks. Last business here was antique restoration. You wouldn't believe the sheer amount of obscure crap they had. Furniture was one thing, but the clutter was something else. Books and knick-knacks and whatnot. We had a lot of trouble getting those guys to move all the machinery out. Spent a good four or five months on emptying this floor alone. They left eventually, but they never came back for this stuff. We should probably get rid of it at some point."

"Huh."

The animal's glass eyes were unnerving. Theoni covered it again. The plastic sheets rustled as she pulled them, and for a second she thought she caught a muffled screech echoing from somewhere distant. She waited, alarmed—there it was once more, this time clear enough that she suppressed a gasp: a shriek from below, hollow, subdued. She'd learned long ago to trust the hearing aid—

she touched it instinctively, making sure her hair still kept it hidden. Theoni turned around stone-faced. A third phantom wail hit her, followed by short, snapping noises, something like voices. She glanced to her right, trying to locate the source of the sound. A seemingly smaller flight of stairs was at the very rear end of the floor, behind boxes of disintegrating books and mounts of broken chairs, tucked away in the murk. She felt cold droplets of sweat forming at her temples. She shuffled through her papers nervously.

"I can show you the top two floors now if you'd like," said Yorgos.

"I think I've got most of the things I need, for the time being."

"Perfect. And if you have any questions at all, ask away."

"For now, I'm covered." She put her files back in her briefcase, then approached him with hesitation. "Maybe just one question."

"Go ahead."

"There's another basement level?"

His eyes narrowed for a split second. "Not really. I mean, technically, yes. We're using it as a boiler room. We had to update some pre-existing radiators, install an air-conditioning system. It's a mess down there, and half the fixtures don't work. A work in progress." He spoke the way someone does when they're stalling for time.

He rubbed the back of his neck. "How did you figure?"

She pointed to the stairs.

"There's gotta be more, right?"

"My, my. Inspector you are."

Theoni mustered up a fake smile. They fell silent. She could almost hear the violent thump of her heart against her sternum.

Yorgos cleared his throat. "I could use a smoke. Care to join me?"

He produced a packet of Marlboro Reds from his jeans and gestured upwards.

"I'd better not. I'm trying to quit, actually."

"Good for you. Excuse my French, but this shit just gives you grief in the end."

He stood in front of her completely still, calculating.

"I'll only be a minute. I have to sort some papers, then I'll be right with you." She tried her best to sound reassuring.

He lingered. "I should leave you to it, then. I'll be outside."

Theoni waited for the sound of his footsteps to grow faint. When she heard the metal clang of the door, she put her briefcase down and moved cautiously towards the twisting staircase. She gripped the still-curing wood railing and descended. Sensor lights sparked on with every few steps, blinking, buzzing, revealing dozens of electrical enclosures with their front panels ripped off the hinges at the subbasement landing. Exposed cables sprawled vein-like across the dirty marble. Against the freshly painted wall beside the door marked FORBIDDEN ENTRY were stacks of paint supplies, commercial paint buckets, wood stain, mineral spirits, some rags. The air down here was damp, stale, chemical. The sounds came from behind the fire door entrance to the boiler room. Everything in her screamed: *Don't.*

Her palm went over the handle and the latched clicked open. Immediately, the metallic smell of decay hit her hard, overpowering everything else. From the backlit entryway, the boiler room's floor was old concrete, pocked with cracks and chips. There was no light switch in here, so she turned her phone's flashlight on and shined it around, but the dark was deep. Theoni thought she saw a cat's eyes reflect but dismissed it as a trick of the brain. She thought about lighting a cigarette to numb her nose from the smell, but stopped dead, hearing a rustle from her hearing aid. "Is someone down here?"

She glanced back the way she'd come, at an oblong light carved into pitch blackness, and her feet crunched over something. She shined the light down at her feet and saw what looked like . . . teeth? No, couldn't be—she was just giving herself the creeps. She'd been in basements like this plenty of times before. Assured herself it was just debris. Theoni turned up the brightness on her phone's light and heard movement through her hearing aid. It seemed all around her for a moment then everything was still. She shined the light around, couldn't find the edges of the boiler room. She followed the sounds and found an old iron furnace. At its mouth were piles of shredded, dirty rags . . . clothes? Like offerings to some terrible shrine. She took two steps and almost slipped on something. Shined the light down again. *Blood.* Further ahead, wet bones, a torso, skulls, a jawbone . . . blood all over the floor, a grotesque trail of sludge. . . It looked like someone had been torn apart Theoni was instantly dizzy, felt like throwing up. She put her hand over her mouth and gagged. Felt her legs quiver at first, then fell forward without realizing, as if someone had taken a baseball bat to the back of her knees. "Fuck, fuck. . ."

"Now, now. I told you it was a mess down here." His voice so loud she winced and scrambled to adjust her hearing aid's volume back to normal. Yorgos sounded different, brighter, the way it does when someone's smiling. "You really should have come out for a cigarette."

"Wh-what is this . . . ?"

Dozens of vicious whispers from the corners filled the room, growing louder, shriller:

"Bring us more . . ."

"Feed us . . ."

"More . . ."

"More . . ."

Theoni feeling her heart race now. She kept her head down, almost at a kneel.

"You couldn't have made this easier? They just want the *invisible ones* to feed on, the ones no one will miss. Those fucking mongrels come here from all over, so why not? Why not offer a hecatomb to these gods? You should be thanking them." Yorgos grabbed her by the hair. "Instead you choose to work on behalf of tribute, of . . . *food.*"

Everything suddenly claustrophobic. She could make out the vague shape of Yorgos standing in front of her, the bodies of whatever they were, emerging around the two of them, grunting, hissing, their sounds raspy like feral animals. She gripped her phone tightly and swung at where she thought his testicles might be, the only thing she knew to do. Connected hard. She grabbed, twisted. Yorgos yelped and fell over, pulling her off balance on top of him. She hit him again, this time in the face, hammering where she thought his were eyes with the edge of her phone and his grip eased. "You fucking bitch—!" he screamed.

Theoni scrambled to her feet, blindly shining the phone around her, almost like a ward. She caught a look at one of them, transfixed by its impossible, wide open mouth, uneven rows of overgrown canines. Its impossibly pale, veiny skin. It winced at the light. She made for the doorway, feeling a sudden sharpness at her side, another at her leg. Theoni kept running and stumbled right into the light, crashing forward against an electrical enclosure. She looked down at her leg, touched her hip, she was bleeding. Shallow scratches, throbbing warm. She'd only just been out of reach. Behind her, just beyond the reach of the light, the inhuman growls. Beyond them: "I'll fucking. . ." He coughed, "fucking kill you myself!"

She slammed the fire door shut. Everything seemed to be moving impossibly slow. She looked around the room for something, anything, and saw the commercial paint buckets. They were too heavy to carry over, so she pushed them against the door, managed to get them wedged up under the handle. It rattled from the other side but didn't open. She blinked, tried to center herself. Patted her breast pocket, remembered the lighter. Yorgos was kicking at the door now. She tried to pry the lid from a bucket of stain. Bent a fingernail and grimaced. It finally came loose, and she pushed it over, sending liters of stain pooling across the floor. She picked up a rag from the piled of supplies, still damp, and it occurred to her: had those been the remains of the contractors? She lit the rag and tossed it on the floor, then limped toward the stairwell. The latch finally gave, and the door cracked open slightly. Yorgos' hand emerged from the door, trying to leverage the wall to push through. The fire began to spread along the floor, small tongues of terror, and reached the electrical enclosure. . . He croaked, "You—" Electricity arced across the fire and the power went out. Yorgos screamed.

Theoni ran from the heat, coughed at the rapid emergence of smoke. The creatures shrieked somewhere behind her. Light from the phone was all but useless in the unlit building, but she ran anyway, trying to remember the tour she'd just taken with . . . *Yorgos*. What the fuck was all this? Her shin hit the corner of something, and she cried out and almost lost her balance. Soon she found the main stairwell, found her way towards a thin mist of daylight coming in through the ground floor's windows. . . .

Theoni Hadzis burst through the entrance, hobbling, and shoved a drunken teenager out of the way. "Oh my god," she said, looking around at the street. The teenager yelled something at her, but she didn't register it and the group he was with kept walking down the street. The homeless man she'd seen earlier eyed her suspiciously, then continued to ramble about something. Theoni turned back toward the entrance and stared at it, expecting Yorgos or those things, those . . . he'd referred to them as gods, but they'd been monsters . . . to emerge from it at any moment as the dusk began to settle in, but they didn't. Instead, she smelled smoke, could hear the faint crackle of a fire within the building. Her phone had left an indentation in her palm from being gripped so tightly. Theoni weakly found the cigarette pack in her chest pocket, hands shaking. She tore the pull tab off. Drew and lit a cigarette and began to walk. She only turned back once and saw the funnel of smoke from behind the building. Theoni exhaled her own. Stared at the sidewalk and walked toward her hotel. The bleeding had slowed, but she'd need to wrap the wounds.

She wandered back in a trance. Reception was deserted; no one there to witness her condition. Nothing seemed real or true anymore. The colors of the streetlights had dulled into a fuzzy haze. She locked herself in the room and could still faintly smell smoke, though maybe she was imagining it, maybe she'd imagined all of it, but the scratches didn't give her that out. . .

The window fogged up with her breath as she listened to the fire engine pass, then the police a few minutes later. "Good," she muttered, staying there a while pressed against the glass, unable to move. She was exhausted. Exhausted by crisis and grief and disbelief. And now fascist fucking vampires? The country wasn't going to hell, it was already there. What else?

Theoni woke up a sweaty mess from an eerily dreamless sleep. She showered and cried and cleaned the scratches and scrapes, then gathered her things and checked out. The receptionist offered to call her a taxi, but she would have had to take it from Egnatia, with the street being closed off because of the fire and all. . . She stopped him before he could finish, thanked him, hurriedly walked out. Once she'd reached the corner, the suitcase rattling loudly against the bumpy sidewalk the whole way, she reached into her chest pocket. She crushed the rest of the pack in her fist and threw its crumpled remains into a garbage bin and began walking toward the highway.

Bomb Thrower
Jo Quenell

The tightness in his chest ceased once reaching Pullman, but his shakes remained. James Upton parked outside his house, killed the ignition, and exhaled with a shudder. The clock read 5:30. The surrounding neighborhood slept. He surrendered to the headrest and stared at the stain of magenta bleeding into the horizon.

Despite hours having passed, the screams still echoed in his skull.

He dug his burner from his pocket and flipped through contacts. After selecting Sterling's name he pressed send. The phone rang six times before anybody answered.

"I got nervous when you didn't call." The older man sounded well-rested.

"County cops love distracted drivers." James paused to yawn. "Anyway, deed's done. I'm home."

"You're a goddamn hero. You know that?"

James didn't know if he felt particularly heroic.

"Have you followed the news?" Sterling asked.

"Tried to. You know back road reception—static and prayer. Last I heard, they were wondering if it was a gas issue. Fire Marshall wanted the place condemned."

"They're past that. Now it's considered 'malicious.' They won't say terrorism until they know more."

James chewed his lower lip. Sterling sensed worry and corrected course.

"Don't sweat yet. We're safe, for now. We have allies spreading stories already, pointing blame elsewhere. The narrative's on our side for the time being."

The armchair lilt in Sterling's voice made James's teeth hurt. He didn't feel any calmer.

"So . . ." he hesitated. "What are the numbers?"

"Eleven are down for good. Many more are critical. Think about that, Jamie. Eleven pinkos. You will be legendary."

James's thoughts circled backward. To the moment the dreadlocked girl snubbed her cigarette against the club's bricks, heading inside for the next band. He remembered laughter and the lingering stench of pot in the air as he crossed the street with his parcel. He remembered his greater self begging to turn around.

Legendary, my ass.

"James? James!" Sterling snapped him back to present. "Are you *there?*"

"Yeah . . . yeah, still here."

"Repeat what I said." Sterling's tone could shorten a man two inches.

"I . . ." James tried, failed. "Sorry."

A deep sigh reminded James of his position.

"I *said* lay low, for a while at least. Get rid of the phone today. Go dark. Don't call—I'll get a hold of you when the smoke clears. Remember your alibi and tell nobody, no matter how pilled they are. You're excused from class for a few days. I'll get you makeup work for the others, but you're set for mine. Deal?"

"Sounds good."

"Great. And Jamie?"

"Yeah?"

"Good work. They'll write books about you one day, son. Hail victory."

"Hail victory."

James killed the call and pocketed his phone. He yawned again and rubbed hands across his tired face.

Sirens rang somewhere close. He jolted in his seat, alert once more, pulse pounding in his ears. He weighed options while opening his glove box and withdrawing his revolver. He could either run, barricade inside the house or die in glory right here. None sounded great. He hadn't encountered a single cop on the drive from Seattle . . . of course they'd nab him at home base.

A minute passed and the sirens faded in the distance. James's guts uncoiled. He shook his head, sighing in disbelief.

You made it, you lucky sonofabitch.

He tucked the gun into the waistline of his pants and left the truck, stepping into a crisp fall morning. He waved to a pretty jogger while approaching the only house on the block free of leftist propaganda.

His hands still shook.

Stale smoke clung to the walls. Some fucker lit up in the house again. His roommates had hosted another recruiting rager—alcohol and literature provided by Sterling. Empty beers and leaflets cluttered the living room. James removed cans from hardbound texts resting on the coffee table. Sterling's books, written under a pseudonym, with titles like *White Advocacy 101* and *Solving the Race Problem.* He stacked hate pamphlets into an organized pile beside the books. He draped an abandoned WSU hoodie over a wet carpet stain and re-pinned a fallen fasces flag to the wall.

Yawning, James entered the kitchen. He knew he should sleep, but didn't kid himself. He debated between coffee and beer. After deciding coffee wouldn't help his shakes, he got a Pabst from the fridge. He removed the revolver from his waistband and set it on the table. Sat, drank, and rubbed his nose. Fuck, that smoke *stank.*

He thought about the dreadlocked girl and chewed his lip some more.

To say he'd spiraled was an understatement. He'd long graduated from online threats, separating himself from trolls and cucks. But this was more severe than hanging nooses, or painting '88' on dorm doors.

If they caught him, he'd face worse than restraining orders or expulsion threats.

He wondered what *She-who-won't-be-named* would say if she found out. The thought ached. Words danced through his mind, sloughing off old scabs.

You scare me, James.

He slammed his beer and crunched the can. He needed to untangle his nerves, something drinking into oblivion could solve. He returned to the fridge, gripped its handle, and pulled.

A cacophony of screams spilled through the open door.

Yelling, James staggered backward. Mortified wailing greeted his eardrums like ice picks. He cupped his ears, frozen in shock.

The fridge door swung wide, exposing scorched innards. Something moved inside the charred detritus piled upon its floor. James stared, horrified.

White bone peeked through the cracks of burnt, crisp skin. He could see joints move as the hand flexed its digits, pointing an accusing finger in his direction:

You did this. YOU did this.

The screams worsened. The hand extended from the cinder, revealing the blackened flesh of a wrist. James saw outlines of shitty tattoos under the crust, and beneath the split skin, rare meat. Bit by bit it grew, from forearm to elbow, then bicep to shoulder. It reached out of the fridge's belly, latching its bony fingers onto the corner and pulling. More rose from the refuse.

The sight of hateful eyes freed James from his paralysis. He charged into the fridge door and slammed it with all his strength. The thing inside hissed, but its grip held. Another slam and the fingers exploded into a cloud of ash and bone. The hand shot back into the fridge. The door stayed shut, extinguishing the screams.

James stood in silence, panting. Upstairs, someone stomped across the floor.

"Shut the *fuck* up!" A roommate yelled from the top of the stairs, before storming back to their room and slamming the door.

James cautiously checked the fridge again, only to find things as they should be. No char, no tinder. No corpse. He shut the door and slumped back down at the table, his shakes now a full-body tremor.

I'm fucking losing it, he thought.

Swirls of smoke danced in his peripherals, disappearing as soon as they arrived. The smell intensified—not cigarettes, but fire damage. Underneath the burnt stench he noticed barbecue and singed hair. A medley of putrid odors hid further beneath.

Behind him, something wheezed.

James lurched forward in panic. Whatever lurked behind moved fast, feet slapping against the linoleum. A hand wrapped around his mouth, forcing him back against his chair before he could reach the gun.

"Sit still," his attacker croaked. Its breath smelled like campfire.

A blackened hand reached across his shoulder, grasped his revolver, and turned it on him. The touch of cold steel against his cheek sprouted goose pimples across his flesh.

"Quiet?"

James nodded vehemently.

It released its hold and crept to the chair across from him. Keeping aim, it sat. A plume of smoke left its nostrils upon exhale.

Words failed.

To call her 'overdone' would be generous. Her skin was black crust, save for random ash-dusted splotches of European flesh. Cooked blood coagulated between cracks in the char. Clothes hung off of her in tatters—remnants of a denim vest, a melted polyester shirt, and a patched skirt. Her dreadlocked hair had been burnt down to mangy blond roots.

She unhinged her jaw, opening her mouth impossibly wide. A spiraling chasm filled the space belonging to teeth and tongue. She dropped the revolver into the black hole and shut her mouth, swallowing.

James stared, shell-shocked. She belched smoke before speaking in an emphysemic voice.

"Ever smell a burning body?"

He shook his head.

"I hadn't either, until last night." The sound rising from her ruined larynx was gravel against sandpaper. *"Believe me, you're not missing out.*

It's weird—once the shock wore off and we were scrambling for exits, fighting and tripping over each other, that's when I noticed. Fuck man, it stank worse than anything I've ever smelled before. In the midst of all that panic, all I could think of was how I'd pay my entire savings never to smell it again."

James felt lightheaded.

"Tell me why."

No easy answer came. Any justification inside his head felt null. The single word falling from his mouth sounded stupid, even to him.

"Communists."

She raised a singed eyebrow and stared at him, waiting for more.

One of Sterling's convincing speeches echoed in his mind. He considered parroting its finer points, such as the death tolls of Stalin and Mao. Or about how the US was falling ill to Marxism farcically repackaged as "progress." He could thump his chest, arguing that it was *his* job as an awakened European to stop the red threat.

But arguing with a corpse seemed pointless, so he kept quiet.

"I'm not a fucking communist," she said.

His heart sank to his guts. More strained silence passed between them.

"So you and your boys are Nazis?"

"Not Nazis. Ethno-nationalists. Identitarians, if you want to be precise."

"Shit by any other name is still shit."

He scowled. "What the fuck do you know anyway?"

She skewered him with a glare. "*I know a scared little boy when I see one. Someone who hurts innocent people—people having fun—due to his own misguided fears. How could you do that?*"

Any sort of defense died in his throat. He sat stagnant in the tension.

"*You're so young. Doubt you could even buy beer. What happened to you? What brought you to this?*"

More of Sterling's rhetoric came to mind.

"I smartened up. Learned that the democracy and equality we're raised to accept is bullshit. I've spent my entire life primed to be sorry for slavery and other junk I had nothing to do with. I'm supposed to believe *my* people are responsible for the world's atrocities. I'm supposed to let others persecute *me.*"

Confidence bolstered his voice. He pointed to the window.

"You think the brown kids filling up the neighborhood out there give a shit about me? They don't. They're taking every high-paying job and hauling their families here from Carbombistan. Enrolling mud babies into *our* schools, without even teaching them the right language. How long 'til English is the new Latin? Fuck that. I'm taking America back for those who deserve it."

She watched him, blank-faced, waiting until he finished.

"*Great. You know how to recite a speech.*"

"Fuck it." He bolted from the table, rage blanching his cheeks. Her fiery glare dared him to move further. He weighed options and returned to his seat, quaking.

"Whoever taught you that shit gave you the directions, right?"

James thought of Sterling feeding him words before giving him flyers to hang or literature to plant. Paint cans and a list of DACA Recipient's dorm numbers. A parcel and a club address.

He nodded.

"So why'd you say yes?"

'You never say no to Sterling,' he wanted to say. Instead, he shrugged.

"Ever think that you're a pawn? A fall-guy?"

James frowned. "Not true."

"It is. You're loyal. Expendable. The second you go down, he'll drop you. You're nothing to him."

"No!" he yelled.

She nodded.

He shot up, overturning his chair in the process. She stood with him.

"*You're* nothing!" he screamed. "You don't know jackshit, because you're *not fucking real.* You were collateral; wrong place, wrong time, too bad, so sad. But nothing you say now matters, because you're not—"

"James," she interrupted, stepping closer. He ignored her.

"You're nothing more than a shred of guilt in the back of my mind, guilt I shouldn't even feel since I did *nothing wrong.* I fought for *my* people. *My* interests. I only wish I'd taken out more fucking degenerates, so spare me any—"

She interrupted him with a scream unlike anything he'd ever heard; a chorus of suffering. Her jaw once again dislocated, distending until her chin reached her chest. James stumbled back, stupefied, staring once more into her chasm of a mouth. Dark, fragrant smoke billowed from her maw, flooding the room.

James choked as the opaque exhaust overtook him, burning his eyes and stabbing his lungs. He fumbled blindly, running into the table before tripping over his capsized chair. He met the ground with enough force to lose his remaining breath.

The harrowing screams intensified. The thick smoke walled him off from the surrounding world. His polluted lungs shrieked, and his frenzied mind raced—what the fuck had he learned to do during a fire?

Instinct barked at him to *Get low!*

He lay flat on his stomach, pressing his cheek against the ground. Sure enough, a pocket of untainted air occupied the inches of space above the floor. He choked and gagged while swallowing, continuing until his lungs filled. He blinked the smoke from his eyes, clearing his blurred vision.

Unrefined dread lurched inside his gut.

The cheap linoleum in his kitchen was gone, replaced by cracked checkerboard tiles. Ash turned the white tiles dishwater gray. The smoke around him decreased and James saw what looked like piles on the ground.

The screams stopped as the remaining smoke dissipated. James lay alone in the middle of a death house.

The inside of the club was little more than a burnt-out husk. Windows shattered, olive-green walls blackened. In the far corner sat fire-damaged pinball tables. Opposite the machines were the remains of a wooden stage. And all along the ground, bodies. Some were whole; others overcooked scraps.

James felt nauseous. It looked like a warzone from some documentary. This didn't happen here.

A counter ran down the right wall, its damaged top littered with shards from exploding pints. All but one of the vinyl-coated stools surrounding the bar top had melted. Above it all hung a TV, its screen miraculously aglow.

"Now Mr. Sterling, it seems—"

"Please," said a familiar voice. "It's Professor Sterling."

James overstepped the surrounding carnage and sat on the remaining bar stool. He stared at the TV.

The screen split. On the left, a dark-skinned reporter sat in a news studio. Sterling stood on the right, dapper in a three-piece suit. A light wind outside the campus tousled his salt and pepper hair. He adjusted a flag pin on his lapel.

"Sorry, *Professor* Sterling. Critics have pointed to you and your organization as the root of Mr. Upton's radicalization. How do you respond to this?"

Sterling smirked. "Clearly it's a smear. A mistruth spread by campus Leftists afraid of good old discourse. Young Americans for Liberty are explicit in our disavowal of Fascism, Nazism, or any sort of political violence."

James's face heated.

"But Professor Sterling, you knew Mr. Upton well, right? Not just from your club, but as a student in your course?"

"I wouldn't say I knew him *well*, per se. Yes, he took my civics course. But you must understand, it's a large class. I don't get to know many students. Mr. Upton's work was unremarkable—he was never more than a name and face to me."

James chewed at his lip until he tasted blood. He clenched fists to quell their tremble.

"Bullshit," he murmured.

"And as for Young Americans? Early on, we had to ask Mr. Upton to distance himself from us. While his radical beliefs are his God-given right, they are not representative of us. Clearly Mr. Upton is a disturbed young man. It's unfortunate he didn't seek help before committing such a terrible act."

"Bullshit!" James yelled.

"We have photos of Mr. Upton mingling with your organization only weeks before the tragedy. It seems there's a mutual camaraderie amongst everybody involved." Said photo flashed across the screen—James with his roommates and others on campus. Some held signs. James passed out literature to whites who fit the part. "Care to comment on *this?*"

"Well, it is a *free speech* rally. Mr. Upton is welcome to his beliefs, no matter how deplorable they may be." Sterling fiddled with his flag pin and cleared his throat. "You know, there wasn't a single news camera when Young Americans helped clean the Hanford Superfund last year. Nor was there any when we held veteran's health fundraisers this past spring. Why is it that as soon as a wingnut—an *unaffiliated* wingnut, to be exact, commits some atrocity, all eyes fall on us? How many times do I have to denounce James Upton, and white supremacy as a whole, before anybody listens?"

The newscaster shuffled his papers. "Thank you, Professor Sterling. I'm sure hearing from you will comfort many on campus. Anything else to add?"

"Nothing at all."

The newscaster thanked Sterling once more and transitioned to a new story. Screaming, James slammed his fists into the glass speckling the bar top. He punched until rage no longer numbed the pain. He blurted profanities at the top of his lungs until his voice wavered. Laying his face into his bloody hands, he sobbed.

"You scare me, James," a familiar voice whispered into his ear.

Yelping, he spun around on his stool, thrusting his gored hands in defense. Bright light stung his eyes. The bar's burnt interior disappeared, as did the bodies. The familiar sight of his kitchen greeted him.

The woman remained across from him, exhaling smoke signals. She watched him, waiting.

"He's lying," James muttered, shaking. He stared at the glass piercing his throbbing hands. Crimson rivulets snaked down his forearms. "He's so full of shit."

She nodded. "*Most figureheads are.*"

He wiped snot from his nose with his wrist. "I . . . I nearly backed out, at the last minute. I should've. I wanted to. But . . . I thought of what he'd say, and . . ." Shaking, he emitted something between a shudder and a sob. "Oh fuck, I knew it was wrong. I'm sorry, okay? I'm so, so sorry . . ."

Something akin to sympathy crossed her face.

"*James. What brought you to this?*"

He paused, straightening, staring at the blood collecting on the table from his hands.

"When I joined, it was . . . I dunno. It made sense. They were the only group on campus that wasn't Left. And at the start it was only about free speech, honoring amendments, shit like that. We weren't doing anything wrong, but the fact that we even existed was so triggering to people . . ." he chuckled humorlessly. "It was fun, I guess."

"*So what changed?*"

He paused again, chewing his lip. "You know the name, 'Corey Willis?'"

She shook her head.

"Black student. Got beat up by a campus cop who said he'd seen him selling drugs at the Student Union. Ended up with permanent brain damage. Campus let the cop go, and the family pressed charges. School went nuts after the acquittal. Protestors shut down classes for a week, blocking lecture halls, rioting like animals.

"When we didn't have a place on campus to meet, Sterling invited us to his house. It was hush-hush, obviously. He gave us beer, even though the oldest of us was only twenty. We first saw him fume, claiming these communists were violating our right to education over the wellbeing of some *thug*. And that it was up to us to fight for common sense, for order. So we held our own rallies. The way the normies reacted to us made me figure we were on to something."

"Still seems a way off from murder."

"Sterling handpicked the loudest of us for an inner circle. Things shifted from communism to race. He made us read his books, invited speakers to lecture us about Eugenics. Then he started with the assignments. Whatever he said, we did. No question."

"But what made you the one to kill?" she asked. *"What drove you?"*

He paused, staring at the table. Memories bubbled upward, their sting still sharp. Crisp November air, nowhere close to cooling the hot hurt he felt inside. Her, disappearing into the late fall night, not looking back even once.

His heart broke. His rage kindled.

"Her name was Amina."

A pregnant silence passed before he spoke again.

"When I joined the rallies . . . she hated it. We'd always had differences, but . . . when I started spending more time with Sterling, she said I changed. That who I'd become scared her. She wondered how long it'd be before I set sights on *her.* She said . . . she said she didn't know how to love the new me." He shrugged. "So she left."

"Did you ever try to fix it?"

"I . . . didn't know how, I guess. I was hurt, yeah, but I was fucking livid, too. I'd been living with her. Suddenly, I was out of a place. So I turned to Sterling. He flipped when he found out who she was, *what* she was. Said I'd risked 'losing myself to degeneracy.' But he still helped me. Got me a room here, under the condition that I'd help recruit." He stared at his bloody hands. "He made me promise to never see her again. Told me at some point, I'd owe him a big favor; something to prove my commitment to the movement." He smirked spitefully. "And now here I am."

"Do you still love her?"

". . . Yeah."

"And what do you think she'll say, once she hears what you've done?"

He shook his head. "I can't even fucking think about it."

More silence. She studied him for a while.

"So what are you going to do about it?"

He shrugged. "Dunno. If I still had the gun I could eat a bullet. How's that for justice served?"

She shook her head. *"That's not justice,"* she rasped. *"It's a temporary solution. There will always be another you, someone else angry enough to declare allegiance. To serve justice, you have to kill the monster for good. That means going for its head. Understand?"*

He frowned.

"I'm saying there's a way to make this right. You've done something horrible. Something you can't take back. But redemption's not lost. You can still prove to the world you're not like them." She pointed upstairs, to where his roommates slept. *"Most of all you'll show her that, no matter what you've done, you were never fully lost. The evil didn't win. Do you want that, James?"*

He considered, then nodded.

"More than anything."

She stood from the chair and approached him. Peeling off her burnt jacket, she dropped it to the floor. Next she grabbed her scorched shirt by the hem and lifted it past her waist, then over her head. Layers of skin went too, flaying from her torso with wet rips. She ignored it, pulling her shirt all the way off. The pink, moist meat of her midsection was raw in spots, overdone in others. A long cavern puckered along her side, its perimeter coated with dried blood. She took firm hold of James's right wrist and led his hand toward the crevice, grunting as she slid his fingers in. His stomach rioted over the feel of slimy warmth, but he didn't fight.

She guided his arm further and further, until he was elbow-deep. His fingers grazed something cold and hard.

"Grab it," she said. *"Take it."*

He fumbled with the object, wrapping his hand around its cylindrical base. He pulled to no success. She urged him between small gasps of discomfort. He complied, tugging harder. It loosened, then freed, threatening to slip from his hands. His arm left her side with a wet slurp. Clumps of bile and black bits dripped from his skin to the floor.

As he examined the familiar object in his hands, a slight smile crossed his mouth.

She leaned close to him, placing hands onto his shoulders.

"*Here's what to do,*" she said.

•

James stepped out of the house and into a world basking in cloudless sunlight. The object weighed his sweatshirt pocket as he trekked across the lawn toward his truck. He no longer chewed his lip.

The smoke clung to his clothes. He had ample time before anybody else caught on. He'd disabled the smoke detectors, and before departing, she'd visited his roommates. He assembled the kindling to a soundtrack of screams.

He'd ensured the burn in the living room was steady before leaving. The flames had spread from the mountain of flags, flyers and books to the carpet and furniture. The house of hate Sterling helped erect would soon be cinder.

Once behind the wheel, he removed the object from his pocket. He examined it, remembering her parting directions. He thought about Amina, then Sterling.

He'd considered calling, but decided a surprise was in order. He imagined the look of annoyance on Sterling's face upon his arrival. That look twisting into horror upon realization of their fate, and the fate of the whole movement. Everything either up in flames or buried in blasted mortar.

James placed the pipe bomb on the passenger seat and dug for his keys. *This is for everything*, he thought, firing up the truck's engine and starting for Sterling's.

His hands were steady the entire drive.

Wedding Bells Strike Thirteen
Violet LeVoit

He never told anyone, but the only way his commute on the cacophonous and dark Broad Street Line was made the slightest bit bearable every grim November morning, with the sun blotted out from war dust as thick as iron shavings and the solstice tilt of the earth, was by closing his eyes and thinking about liquid soap dispensers. He lusted after all of them—upper-crust snobbish ones, their cylindrical brushed steel bodies and hummingbird proboscis nozzle betraying just the tiniest, sauciest bead of silky treasure dripping at the tip. Fresh and innocent gamine porcelain ones, their sculpted curlicues pressing demurely against his hands as he gripped their petite bodies and coaxed, enticed, seduced their shy permission to be the first to depress their plunger and watch the ecstatic splurt of their pearly, perfumed payload drool down their unstained body, a virgin made naughty and shameless by what he imagined to be the repressed carnality he'd awakened inside. And the streetwalkers: the 99 cent disposable ones crowding the low bodega shelf, their crassly transparent bodies making no bones about the brazenly dyed treat they held inside, or how willing they would be to give it up as he plunged them again and again with rough pounding strokes, squirting their cheap detergent over his naked body and stroking their smooth polyethylene shells against his erection before splattering them with his own sticky spunk and throwing their spent shell in the trash. He thought about this with his coat bunched high over his groin so no one could see the swell against his fly, and he quelled his thoughts like clockwork by 15th Street Station so he could exit at 8th without reproach. He dreaded 15th Street.

He made his small devotions at the altar of his office cubicle: coffee, a scan of the blogs, a resigned sigh when the timer in the corner of the screen nagged him to get to work. He pulled up the queue and scanned today's list.

Vacuum Cleaner Sluts
Wide-Screen TV Whores Get Nasty
My Brand-Name Breakfast Cereals Want to Fuck!
Ass-Craving 2-ply Toilet Paper
18yo Balsamic Vinegar's First Time
Grind that Pepper Mill!
Back Door Screen Action
3-way Lightbulbs

Bodacious Cigarette Butts
Naughty MILF Welcome Mats
Daddy Goes Down Safety-Grip Stairs
Stepsiblings Love Non-Toxic Markers
Paper Clips Like to Watch
Sink Drains Get Stuffed with 18" Snakes
Hot Coed Dorm Refrigerators

He had four descriptions to write for each: 256 characters, 99 characters, 59 characters, a mere 27. That's what lonely guys like him would read while coasting through their on-screen program guides tonight when they got home from their equally uninspiring jobs. He'd stopped being creative with the descriptions years ago. He had a list of reusable adjectives on his desk: naughty, sassy, saucy, randy, horny. "Uninhibited" was too long, it was a waste of precious letters. "Shameless," too. He had another list of codas: get nasty, at play, get wild, go nuts, bare all. He plowed through the list in the numb daze he'd grown over the years, like a callous.

Dust suckers get nasty.
Wide screen TVs at play.
Breakfast cereal goes nuts.
Toilet paper gets used.
Virgin vinegar goes bad.
Hot pepper grinding action.
Slammin' back door screens.
Lightbulbs swing both ways.
Sassy cigarette butts.
Hardcore welcome mats.

Daddies take the stairs.
Markers bust taboos.
Voyeuristic office supplies.
Sweet sink drains get drilled.
Refrigerators get hot.

Masterpieces of pornographic haiku, all of them. The list scrolled on and on. He'd been doing this for so many years that the warning timer at the corner of the screen never once dissolved to red for lingering on a record for too long. An hour in he wearied, and when words failed he wrote:

The title says it all.

He was just about to log off when one more movie burst into the queue. For a moment his heart leapt.

Hand Sanitizers
Get Dirty

It stirred nothing in him. Not close enough. In the eight years he'd worked here, he'd never seen a liquid soap dispenser movie come through the queue. All the other movies sounded ridiculous to his libido. Who could possibly get turned on by watching envelopes ripped open? By the sound of an electric can opener doing its thing on a can of baked beans? How could a household item as ubiquitous as soap dispensers go forgotten? A movie came through the other day for those disposable plastic slip covers they put over digital thermometers. He watched the excerpt. The camera lovingly coasted over the seam where the two edges of the slip cover met. "You're gonna be so rough under my tongue," a voice purred. "Oooh, that soft little pocket of mine is gonna get torn up. I don't know if I can wait the full 30 seconds for the beep with your big rough disposable digital thermometer guard so deep in there."

He sighed and dashed off:

Cleaning dirty situations.

Today was all consumer porn. Yesterday it was policy porn. *Foreigners Get Their Assholes Wrecked. Hardcore Church-on-State Action. Trade Exclusionist Hotties. Keep My Borders Safe!* And the Victor, always, the daily address of him thrusting again and again into some hapless unlucky while he bloviates about The Good Old Days we are all returning to. Thinking about having to watch that again tonight called for more coffee. At least the coffee was free.

He sat back down. The queue had respawned with more titles.

12" Frying Pans Get Hot
All-Squirting Garden Hose Action
Sp. 8yo F

The last one puzzled him. He pulled up the excerpt and his blood froze. Not a consumer product. An eight-year-old girl, hair plaited, tiny butt cheeks bare, laid across the anonymous shiny quilt of a motel bedspread, and a nude man—

He swallowed hard. He shut the excerpt off and jumped out of his chair. His supervisor was sitting in her office. "I need you to see something," he gasped.

She followed him to his cubicle. He hesitated. "This is bad," he said, and clicked on the excerpt again. She watched the girl, the bedspread, the dangle of the perpetrator's genitals. "Don't worry about it," she said.

"How can you say that?"

"It's archival footage. All pornography is state property. This just got caught in the mix. Just write "archival" in the description and be done with it. It'll be flagged and won't ever be shown."

"Can't we just delete it?" The excerpt was still running, past the point he had shut it off, and the crack of the spankings and the girl's anguished and sincere "no"s were digging barbs into him.

She shook her head. "We can't destroy government property." She saw his distress and clicked the excerpt off. "I know it's unpleasant dealing with these. You won't get many." She left. He took a sip of coffee. It did nothing for his blood pressure.

His aftershock was interrupted by a pink ticket rocketing through the memo slot at the back of his desk, lolling like a panting dog's tongue, making him jump. He ripped it off at the base and read its alert, heart sinking. Mother*fucker*. He knew it was only a matter of time. That's what everyone says when they get audited, or drafted, or their dog dies, but what they mean is that it's a matter of someone else's time, that these things never happen to you. Until today. He read it again, head shaking. Not today. Not ever, really, but definitely not today. He sighed, snatched up his jacket and keys, and stomped out of the office.

Back on the fetid, crowded subway, past signs for The Victor—the official ones that read "I LOVE VICTOR," with his smug, sneering portrait, and the unofficial ones, the graffiti, the stickers, the scrawls that read "I HATE VICTOR," "NO VICTOR," "FUCK VICTOR," or just "VICTOR" x'ed out. The unofficial signs outnumbered the official ones ten to one. You could never escape Victor's name. It was scratched into every hard surface on the subway and scribbled onto every window and seat. Fellow riders wore hateful buttons that nevertheless kept the word "VICTOR" fresh in the mind. *Free speech and debate is important*, Victor said about the graffiti in last night's address, as he came all over the face of some migrant cowering on the floor of the Oval Office. *It's an essential constitutional right, and that's why we're not going to take the graffiti down. The people have a voice*, he smiled, a shit-eating, ass-fucking grin. *That's what I've said since the beginning. And I've never lied to you.*

The train only stalled for mechanical delays twice before reaching the big granite Albert Little Institute for Marriage. This was his second visit in his life, and the first time he remembered. He strained at the details of the cavernous main lobby: the metal detectors, the ricocheting echo of every footfall against the smooth dark marble walls and floors and two-story-tall ceiling, the side entrance for mothers and infants. He couldn't spark a recollection of the ten trips he took here in his first year, when a clerk read his time and date of birth from a long dot matrix print-out and confirmed his assigned desire, like a court astrologer declaring a prophecy. Who knows why they chose soap dispensers for him. *How does one even install a desire in an infant*, he wondered, and immediately didn't want to know. In any case, that lonely lust was the only thing he took with him from this building. Everything else about this momentous place he remembered as much as other men remember their circumcisions.

The ticket said Room 101. He took the elevator down. Government buildings have no irony. The narrow, florescent-lit hallway stretching to the vanishing point with anonymous mock-wood doors staring glumly at their spouse across the hall might have been a masterpiece of Late Dystopian architecture, if anyone cared about that sort of thing anymore. He found the office and opened the door towards him. Its width was one tantalizing hair too wide to open completely before jamming on the opposing door's knob. For one claustrophobic moment he was closed in the hall behind it, like an animal in a humane trap. He shut the door to a crack and squeezed by before entering on the other side.

The social worker's office walls were tinged nicotine yellow, and one look at the desk's overflowing ashtray explained why. The social worker had the kind of face that smoking flatters: lean cheeks, square jaw, lizard eyes that darted with the snap of intelligence. The cigarette in between his tight lips was the only thing that flattered him, since he wore the government worker's uniform of a wide dung-brown tie and a short-sleeved button-down shirt the same color as the stained walls. Of all the ways to survive a bureaucracy, he'd chosen camouflage. He saw the slip in his visitor's hands. "Mazeltov," he said. "Have a seat."

"Your wife," the social worker said with a weary exhale as he handed him a stack of papers from the disarray of his desk, "is sixteen years old. She's got strawberry blonde hair, a baby face, and a laryngectomy."

"What's a laryngectomy?"

"She talks with one of those boxes cancer patients get when they get their throat removed." He held his fist to his Adam's apple. "You-know-like-this" he said through his nose in a monotone robot whine.

"Does she have cancer?"

"No. Although she is under quarantine. She's pre-converted." He made a tsk click. "Dad, and step-brother. It's an ugly case, but it's over now. There's a photo." It's true, there was one, a black-and-white one paperclipped in the stack. "Baby face" was charitable. She had broad, too-fat cheeks that squeezed out her raisin-sized eyes, eyebrows so pale they were invisible, a frizzy ponytail, a thin frown. Her head was ducked slightly down, as if the camera was chastising her. The gesture only partially hid the keloid scar spanning her neck, and the whitish plastic plug stopping up the hole in her throat. "They weren't strangers, so her quarantine should be over pretty quickly."

Something about the unacceptability of this fate rose up in him. "I'm in love with soap dispensers," he protested.

The social worker sighed. "What do you want me to do? You and everybody else who comes in here. They've all got something assigned—paper towels, dog food, those safety covers that go over electrical sockets—that's a big one, I see that all the time. Go figure. And they all say the same thing, that they can't love someone who isn't a safety plug, how can you do this to me, and I see them a year later and they've got a kid and they're making it work. You learn, is what I'm saying."

"Are you married?

The social worker fixed him with a look. "I was," he said. He leaned back, measuring something in his audience with calculating eyes. "My wife died," he finally said, "of cervical cancer. And now I am designated Quarantine Under Review."

It was a hell of an admission, and its nakedness humbled him. "Sorry to ask," he mumbled. "You know, I have cavities—" he confessed, and then immediately regretted how narcissistic it sounded. The quarantine for tooth decay bacteria was just a set of guidelines—no kissing, no sharing soda or bites of food, government-supplied antibacterial toothbrushes. Not like having AIDS. Or hepatitis. Or Satoshi's necrosis. It wasn't the life of someone with a viral cancer. "Under review" was a bureaucratic nicety for "forever". "I'm sorry," he said, and clammed up.

The social worker looked at him hard with those canny lizard eyes. "Thank you," he finally said. He picked up another sheaf of papers and inhaled sharply to speak before he was cut off. "What was her name?"

The social worker stopped in mid-breath. "Debra," he said.

"Were you arranged?"

"No. We met."

"I know it's personal, but . . . How did you find a way around . . . you know . . . her deal, and your deal—"

"We didn't have deals." He put the papers down. "We were born in the last year of babies that weren't assigned a consumer fetish."

"So your product was each other."

A twisted little smile flickered pain across his face for a moment. "I guess that's the only way people your age can think about it now, but I guess you're right."

A thought ached at him, a feeling that had floated around inside him in feathery shards his whole life but had never been given the gift of tongues before this moment. "I don't know why they only made one of me," he said, in a voice more anguished than he intended. "I mean,

I know why—they pick it for you if they think they're going to need to sell a lot of them in 13 years. And for seven minutes they thought they would need to sell soap dispensers, and then seven minutes later they changed their minds. And here I am—the only one."

"You're not, actually," said the social worker, flipping open a manila folder. "Yeah, there's one more. A woman."

"What?" The news scalded his ears. "Where? What's her name?"

"Doesn't say. Looks like she left with her family to Nowy Lodz before the war." Closes folder. "That's all we got."

"How'd she escape?"

The social worker sucked the air in between his teeth. "You know, stay away from that word, if you're smart. We don't use it. Because there's nothing here to escape." He pointed to the speaker on the wall, to the big red button on the desk, to the four vacant corners of the drop ceiling where a profoundly subtle surveillance technology stayed hidden. He picked up a pen and signed his name to the marriage form and tore off two of the triplicates before sliding the middle yellow slip across the table to him. "Your wife's name is Alice. You get a paid day off to get acquainted, starting now. What time is it?" He squinted at a clock on the opposite wall. "Yikes, almost four. You've got to go pick her up at the depot. Come back tomorrow, we'll go over the other stuff then. Oh, and—" The social worker reached into a low drawer and dropped two aluminum vials and two fierce glass hypodermics onto the desk. "Happy honeymoon."

He didn't think about soap dispensers once on the subway. His mind swam with this woman in Nowy Lodz, someone else with his fetish in the world. He imagined her with thick dark wiry hair of a wildness and length not often seen, and tan skin, and laughing eyes, and a long-toothed smile that could brighten even a skull. Her stomach was a soft carved-out spoon dotted with a dark dab of navel, and her breasts were all thumbtack nipple. He imagined liquid soap coursing down them in thick honey cascades of blue and pink and green, her tongue slurping eagerly at the nozzle, and the way she put her hand to her mouth like a giggly schoolgirl when a burp burst a mouthful of bubbles free, floating them high in the air like his delight made manifest. Laughing and laughing, squirting herself all over. She didn't ridicule him or wrinkle her nose in revulsion when he rubbed himself with the soaped-up bottle or slid it, slick, against the crack of her ass. To the contrary: she delighted in squirting the softest, most moisturized soap all over his dick, stroking it with her slim fingers, gasping and purring in wonder as they both stared at each other's eyes through the distorting plastic of a spent economy-sized dispenser. The social worker had given him the vials of chemsex as the standard matrimonial bonus. Before, he'd thought he'd just sell them on the black market instead of squandering them on his "honeymoon". Now he considered illegally hoarding them, injecting them all himself while dreaming of Nowylodzia, that must be her name, his real wife, the orgasm he'd have while shot up with a double rush of with chemsex a magic charm to bring her closer. She must be so lonely, too.

His giddy reverie died at the bride depot. The building was designed with livestock in mind, and looked like it was decorated by a romance novelist. There were sprays of plastic lilacs everywhere. He handed his slip to the woman behind the window in the wall and stood outside in the stockyard behind the lavender velvet ropes, waiting for Alice. It started drizzling a little.

She came out from under the corrugated steel awning of the depot dormitory clutching her cardboard dowry box. She waddled a little when she walked, and her legs had that curious bowed-in quality that terminally fat people have. She kept her head down, looking only at the next few steps ahead on the wet concrete tarmac. Her box was freckled with tan raindrop spatters by the time she got to him.

"Hello," he said. Her laryngectomy stoma was horrifying. Every time she swallowed, the white plastic plug jumped in her throat, and its irritated circumference was wet with serum and mucus. She must have felt him staring, and wiped at its edges reflexively. She stood there, paralyzed, and finally raised the black cylinder of her electrolarynx to her throat. "Hello," the box buzzed.

He paid for her token and on the subway ride home thought only of Nowylodzia. He could not bring himself to put any attention on the sad creature who hunched next to him, arms crossed tightly over the lump that encompassed both belly and chest underneath her puffy windbreaker. She was not whom he was destined for and they both knew it. The accumulated guilt of his rudeness rushed over him when the subway *bing-bonged* their stop. "Here, let me carry that for you," he said, reaching for her dowry box, and was shocked to discover it was as light as if it were empty.

He pondered offering to carry her over the threshold when they arrived at his apartment, and thought better of it. "Here we are," he said, flicking on the light, and was instantly mortified by how many empty soap dispensers he'd left lying around the place. "Sorry. Sorry," he said, scrambling to gather up his shame. "If I'd know I was getting married today, I would have straightened up a little. It's just my assigned fetish," he said by way of apology, his frantic arms full of soap bottle mistresses. She said nothing to this, only watched him scurry around the room with her thousand-yard stare. He dumped them in the recycling and came back to the room, panting.

"Is there anything you'd like? Some water?" She shook her head. He racked his brain for a next conversational tactic. "Want a tour?" She nodded. "Well, here's the kitchen—" He turned on the light and waved at the closet-sized space. "And a living room, where we are now. And here's the bathroom, and . . . I guess it's now *our* bedroom." He opened the door and was chagrined again to see his usual bachelor squalor through her eyes. And more soap bottles everywhere, dammit. "I'll clear you a drawer," he said, and scooped out all of his socks from the top drawer of the dresser. "There you are. Go ahead," he nodded. She picked up her dowry box. It was bound with cellophane tape. She clawed at it with her stubby fingernails for a moment before he stepped forward and punctured it with his key. She made the tiniest, airiest grunt of sound that must have been thanks, and opened it. Inside was a single change of clothing and *Wifely Duties in Marriage*, the standard copy. She placed both inside the drawer with such care that it stirred his heart for a moment.

"What do you like to eat? Come on, you have to tell me," he teased, although mostly he was tired of playing a guessing game with this voiceless sphinx. She put her electrolarynx to her throat. "I like . . ." The buzz trailed off, as if she was gathering courage. "I like mashed potatoes."

"Do you like French fries? Ketchup?"

She shook her head no with a sudden shudder.

"Toast? Butter? Jam?"

A gentler headshake no. "Too hard," she buzzed.

"I have vegetable soup. I have a chocolate peanut butter ice cream pie in the freezer, too."

He saw something brighten in her eyes. "Okay."

At dinner she chewed every soft mouthful of soup methodically, as if it might have a fish bone in it, and swallowed with a sip of water, lifting her chin like a bird to dribble it down her throat. He tried not to look at her too much and instead dabbed his ketchup around on his plate in impressionistic swirls. Her eyes shone when he sliced the pie. She waited until the ice cream was very soft and velvety before putting it in her mouth. and chewed each forkful with careful strokes. There was a graciousness to how she ate that struck him as rare, and refined, despite the way the plug jumped in her neck with each swallow.

After dinner they threw away the plates and settled in the living room to watch The Victor's address. Tonight he was forcing a septuagenarian to fellate him while he explained the new tax plan. *You're going to save so much money*, he crowed over her gagging sounds. Alice sat beside him on the couch, watching the broadcast stoically. She got up to use the bathroom twice. On her second absence he reflected on how if she hadn't been there he'd be squirting a soap bottle absentmindedly while stroking himself, the same way he got through every mandatory viewing of The Victor's nightly address. He pondered if he had enough time to rub out a quick one when the toilet flushed and she re-entered the room.

She was completely naked, except for her socks, and she stood before him, head bowed, belly out. Her body was a lumpy mess, pockmarked with cellulite and stained here and there with soft blue bruises. All of her mass was packed in above her hips in a huge stomach and fat forearms that teetered on legs that tapered down to tiny feet. She had the silhouette of an ice cream cone packed with a scoop of instant mashed potatoes. Her breasts were tiny and not likely to get much bigger.

"What are you doing?" he said, shocked. He felt absolutely no desire for her.

She held the electrolarynx to her throat. "I guess . . . it's just time," she buzzed.

"Did you read the wifely book?"

She nodded.

"I mean, we don't have to . . ."

"But we do," she said. "It's the law."

He took a deep breath and exhaled slowly. "All right," he said, slapping his hands on his thighs and forcing himself to stand up off the couch. "I guess I'll get things ready."

He put a saucepan full of water on the stove and took the hypodermics from his bag. She watched as he plunked the needles into the rolling boil and tapped the metal cylinders, looking for the nozzle. When he'd drawn the clean needles full of oily chemsex she put out her arm stoically and didn't wince when the needle beaded ruby blood in the soft crook of her elbow. When it was done she rubbed the spot and didn't say a word as he prepared his own dose. Jesus, why do they have to make these needles so big?

"I guess we'd better lay down," he said, and took off his own clothes. If she had thoughts about the un-ideal state of his chest or gut or penis she kept them to herself. They lay down under the covers and stared at the ceiling and waited.

It hit her first. A creamy slackening washed over her face as her eyes shut and mouth opened in astonished pleasure. He watched in amazement as some invisible network of tension bonds went lax under her skin, releasing the forehead and frown until you could see the tender girl she once was again. He was marveling at the change when a sweeping, prickling wave started the length of his spine and drove itself down into the nerves of his genitals, lighting every one of them up with what he synesthetically felt as a wicked blue luminescence, softly throbbing with the pulse of blood in his veins. "Do you feel that too?" he whispered, astonished, and her mouth moved silently "yes". The places her skin touched his fizzed with champagne bubble warmth. The flesh that had repulsed him a few minutes ago held a new fascination, and his hands leapt out to explore it. He palpated the skin of her belly, feeling the knots of fat underneath the rolling lumps of her hide and the Braille tiger stripes of her stretch marks, as she twisted her stubby fingers around and around his chest hair as if trying to solve a problem hidden within them. He forgot all about his quarantine and moved in to kiss her when the second wave hit, a concupiscent knockout blow so complete it knocked him back against his pillow, the sex urge blown far past the point of an itch to hump and into psychedelic paralysis. His vision flicked with motes of light singing out with the same joy his wife displayed beside him, her body alternately flexing and melting in the grip of the same chemical storm running amok in his veins. As if by previous agreement they locked eyes, NOW, and suddenly he could see the pleading gentleness in every speck of brown and tan and hazel and coffee and chocolate and bronze in the pinpoint specks of her iris, and the swallowing vaginal void of her pupil, inviting him in. He could barely control his omniquivering muscles enough to lift his hand in a single chosen direction, but he did, and when he was able to press it against her cheek and slowly stroke down, the way her eyes closed in relief at his touch tore a hole in the box he'd been keeping all his human feelings inside. The hot slide of his tears down his cheeks sent a quiver down every telegraph line nerve in his body. He saw now how inadequate his fetish was, with its herky-jerky selfish orgasm, and how now all he wanted was to float in the liquid of this hormonal bath forever, with her, his beloved, the one he would protect above all, for all, forever. "Why did I wait?" he whispered, and she tucked her head under his chin and sighed deeply.

They lay there for hours, their respiration slowed by the chemsex, agog. The electrospectral sensations surged and flowed and slowly faded to moth wing flutters as the vibrant indigo of the dark cooled to just plain night. Sleep paralysis made him urinate on her but neither one minded, both of their hearts were so full of forgiveness for every facet of the human condition, every frailty, every humble and sincere endeavor to do good, and we *do* do good, every one of us, God bless us all. Their bones turned to lead and they slept in narcotic bliss.

The next morning he awoke alone in damp sheets, much less hungover than he thought he would be. The sun was streaming in the window from behind the torn laminate shade, and there were soft clinking sounds from the kitchen. He realized how long it had been since he'd heard those gentle chirpy morning sounds: the *tsss* of the tap turning on and off, the bell-like tinkle of spoons stirring coffee. Suddenly he felt a great urgency to not miss out a moment of her puttering around, and leapt to his feet with Christmas morning eagerness while sweeping himself up in a bathrobe.

She was standing up at the stove, wearing the one nightgown her dowry box supplied. It was resolutely frumpy, with a half-hearted fringe of mass-produced lace at the neckline. She was beautiful in it. She looked like a forgotten Vermeer. *Girl Boiling Hypodermics at Dawn.* When she saw him at the doorway, she made the tiniest obeisant duck of her head and shyly presented him with a cup of tea she'd left steeping on the counter, offering it to him formally, both hands trembling. Looking at the white mug in her almost colorlessly peach hands stirred something of tremendous tenderness in him. No soap dispenser, no matter how comely or shameless, had ever made him tea. No imaginary woman, either. He took it gratefully, and only upon touching the quite hot ceramic did he realize what a burden she had borne patiently and politely against her palms.

She lifted the electrolarynx to speak.

"I think we did it wrong," she buzzed. She pointed to the hollow spent cartridges. "There's markings on the sides for seven doses. We took them all in one night," she giggled, hiding her mouth behind her hand.

"You're kidding me," he said, and took a look for himself. "No wonder. I've never heard anyone talk about chemsex that way. They just said it gives them a tingle and takes the edge off."

"Is our marriage consummated now?"

"I don't know." He thought about it. "I guess so?"

"I guess so too." She smiled at the pan's rolling boil.

He put his mug down. "Do you have tea for yourself?"

She shook her head.

"Can I make you some?"

She shook her head again and stayed very still. Something in the air got charged with her quiet. "What, you're a coffee drinker?" he joked nervously, but she didn't move. Finally she lifted the electrolarynx to her throat very slowly, as if it had grown very heavy, and spoke.

"I don't like drinking anything hot."

The pieces were already coming together in his mind but he asked anyway. "Why not?"

She stared into the rolling boil, at the hypodermics clattering around. She turned off the gas.

"Is that why you can't talk?"

She nodded.

"I'm sorry," he said. "I shouldn't have—"

"You're my husband, so I'll tell you," she buzzed, her dark eyes fixed on him with grave clarity. "My father and my stepbrother made me drink hot frying oil. They pre-converted me. A lot."

"That's illegal," he said, horrified. "I mean, even if you're related, they're still violating quarantine—"

"They violated *me*," she said.

And suddenly, in that satori burst of seeing her personhood, not her quarantine status, he realized his wife had carnal knowledge he did not have. No one he knew had it, no matter how much they'd sprayed themselves with laundry starch or licked blister packs of AA batteries or indulged any of their consumer fetishes to the obsessive utmost. She knew what it was like to have raw contact with another human being, in the most shameless, unmediated state between their wet and savage parts, unbetrothed by some corporation, unbrokered by pornography. You let them in your body for good or for ill, and everything inside them poured out into you. Sometimes it was love and sometimes it was hot oil on your soul, and that was the chance you took, when it was real. He knew he shouldn't ask the next question and yet he could not stop himself.

"Do you like . . . I mean . . ."

"I didn't," she said. She was sniffling a little, but he couldn't tell if it was because she was crying or because the boiling water had loosened something in her sinuses. She rubbed her nose on the edge of her hand. "But doing the chemsex changed my mind."

He could barely believe the forms his lips and tongue were making to shape the breath behind the question now coming out of his mouth. "Do you want to try?"

She looked at him for a long time, her eyebrows furrowing up in what was either gratitude or burgeoning tears. Her lips pursed, and she nodded.

His heart pounded as he walked closer to her and rested his arm on her bare shoulder. Her flesh was nothing like a soap dispenser's smooth shell, or the worried skin of her belly. It had a totally unique give, but the spring in its yielding only went so far, and pressing further revealed the firmness of what must be the muscle underneath, and the bone. In an old movie once he had seen an actor grab his leading lady by the forearms and tug her to him. He tried it. It was a strange gesture but maybe it had some truth in it, some small mote of the way men and women used to feel about each other. Maybe it would work for him. Face to face with her he realized he had never been close enough to anyone to be breathing the same air. She reached for her electrolarynx.

"What's your name?" she buzzed.

"Jim," he said. "Well, James. But you can call me Jim."

"Jim," she said. He could hear the wonder in her voice even through the way the electrolarynx stripped the syllable. She made his name sound exotic, a made-up name from a character in a science fiction story, as if he was the only Jim ever born and its strangeness and perfection referred only to glorious him. "Do we kiss?"

He hesitated, thinking about his quarantine. "Do we?"

"Yes," she said, and put the electrolarynx down, and he was stunned again by the give of her lips on his, the way the hard teeth behind them parted and unlocked a surprising space that tasted dark, the welcome flex of her tongue inside, the smell of her cheek pressed so close to his nose. Something lurched up in him, like the way a lethargic house cat leaps to savage purpose at the sight of a mouse, and he seized her at the back of the neck with both hands and fiercely pressed her face closer to him as if trying to cut it in half with his mouth. A galvanic fire shot up and down a dormant lattice of nerves in his body, from crown to groin to millions of pores crying out to be pressed against her skin, and when they were, prone on the bed, her nightgown on the kitchen floor, each one sang out in naked exaltation. He knew what came next in this progression of events, where the gun of his erection revealed in the second act must be placed in the third, and it made his stomach light up with crawling adrenaline. He couldn't breathe as he placed the tip against the wet Rubicon and suddenly, she was a topographic puzzle with an impossible inside and out, that pocket of her mouth was wow, *nothing* compared to this, and that revelation and the slick and the oh-Jesus made everything in the room sing with the *now* sharpness of a suicide in the moment his feet leave the bridge. She grabbed his shoulders with hands that became more and more encouraging as he pumped awkwardly, his hip flexors grown weak from disuse. He buried his face in her neck without thinking about her throat plug. He didn't care. It wasn't as important as the choice chamois pocket right under her earlobe and jaw whose tenderness yearned to be kissed. It didn't matter. *These things don't matter when you're with someone you love*, and with that thought a balance violently tipped and all the phosphorescent pleasure pooling and swirling south of his navel bolted for the exit.

When the daze faded he lifted himself up on an elbow and looked at her.

"Are you okay?" he asked. She nodded. She'd left her electrolarynx in the kitchen.

"You don't have to lie to make me feel better," he said. "You can really tell me." She rolled over and scrambled around for a pen in the nightstand. She found one but couldn't find paper. "It's okay," he said, "I'll just go get your thing from the kitchen," but she started writing on her arm, sticking her tongue out of the corner of her mouth like a kid trying to concentrate. Her handwriting was quavery.

i do and dont but i want to keep doing it

She stopped, then thought better. She added: *with you*

"Okay," he said, and kissed her on the forehead. Thin flesh on smooth bone. *Everywhere on you is different to kiss*, he thought, *and marvelous.*

He went back to Albert Little that afternoon.

"Her quarantine is temporary and conditional, you know," said the social worker. "She's eligible for artificial insemination in a few months." He opened a manila folder. "She's not cleared for vaginal birth, but she can have a grade 1 sterile C-section. You get up to three of those."

"Does it have to be artificial?"

The social worker frowned at his paperwork. "It's preferred," he finally said.

"Well, what does 'preferred' mean?"

"It means the government prefers it." He closed the folder and shrugged, as if he was holding up the invisible, real answer for scrutiny in his upturned palms.

Jim sank back in his chair.

"What if she was already pregnant?"

The social worker raised an eyebrow. "Is she?"

"I mean, what if . . . if before she got to me."

"Then she'll go up to a Grade 2, and we'll just go from there." He looked pointedly at him. "But maybe you're talking about . . . *all* scenarios."

Jim swallowed hard. "Maybe."

"They don't fool around with quarantine, you know that."

"I know."

"I want you to be completely honest with me," he said. "We *are* talking about a hypothetical."

"Yes. I swear to you that I am."

"Because it's only been 24 hours."

"Yes."

"Then I suggest that you cross that bridge if you come to it, and in the meantime don't do anything that will make anyone curious about a cheek or vaginal or urethral or rectal swab." He leaned back. "Give up the big one, and in the meantime get creative. That's not policy. That's *my* advice. To you."

Jim looked up at the corners of the room. "You know, they can hear you."

"I'm well aware of that."

"You're not afraid?"

He smiled a bitter little smile that was almost a frown. "Retirement is in 26 years," he said. "I have no family. I'm considering other options."

They sat for a while in the sad silence. Suicide by surveillance.

"You've been good to me," Jim said.

The social worker gave the softest, bittersweetest snort of air. "You've got a chance to have a family," he said, looking not into Jim's eyes but into the empty corner of the room behind him. "That's a golden ticket. I suggest you take it. All the rest is just inconvenience."

Jim thought about that for a moment: could he just have a family with Alice? She'd be a gentle Madonna, whispering lullabies to their fat-cheeked baby so as not to scare them with the buzz of her electrolarynx. In his gut he knew she'd be tender, no matter what anyone else had taught her about a parent's dominion. And then the day they'd have to take them to Albert Little . . .

No, he couldn't do that to his kid. Hand a baby over to white-suited technicians, watch her disappear through swinging double doors to be inculcated with an unnatural fixation on a consumer product. Condemn her to a life sated with the artificial erotic. Soap dispensers? What was he thinking all those years? *We've got to leave,* he thought. *We'll get out. There's no other way.*

"How's she doing?" the social worker asked. "How are her exams going?"

"Good, I guess," he said. "She doesn't talk about it. I guess she needs to finish her housewife study-at-home degree."

"That's good. She can go back to her high school diploma then." His eyes darted to the clock. "Your 24 hours off is ending in 45 minutes. Come back anytime."

He knew his work was meaningless duty, but now its emptiness resonated like a lone ball bearing bouncing in an airplane hangar. He pitied and resented the horny citizens stuffing their inexhaustible loneliness with:

Down Comforters Get Dirty
Spring Break Keychains
Military Spending MILFS
All-Anal Spice Racks
Squirting Nasty Refrigerator Magnets
Propaganda Gets Me Wet!
12" Sprocket Wrenches
Surveil Me Harder and Deeper
Hardworking Decent White Patriot Sluts

Go Nuts
Chewing Gum Gets Pounded
H.O. 12yo F

Oh, no. He didn't want to know. Every cell in him refused to even open the record. The timer at the corner of the screen was blinking green, fading to yellow, fading to red. If he hesitated they'd know. He saw his boss cast a glance at his desk. Fine. Fine. He'd open it, type "archival" and forget it ever existed.

He opened the record. Someone had already written a description. Shocked, he clicked on the excerpt. It was her. She was so small, her face round and unformed, 50 pounds lighter, eyes pleading but face still broken with betrayal, the kind of shock that only comes when you still trust someone completely. They had the countertop deep fryer's basin. One was holding her cheeks, squeezing them open like giving a cat a pill. She was flailing her thin girlish arms and legs against anything, the table, her stepbrother, the floor. There was a half-eaten plate of French fries and ketchup on the table, and her frantic banging knocked it to the linoleum. In that moment he realized how many videos he'd processed since he'd been there, how there had never been the same woman in any trailer, thousands and thousands of them, and how that must be part of Albert Little—boy babies assigned a fetish, girl babies assigned the movie they'll appear in one day. And once they're broken, they're assigned a husband—and they never question his affection for kitchen towels or air filters or—it burned him to think it—soap dispensers, because they expect nothing more, they don't want what they think is sex anyway, they get seven days of a numbing dose of chemsex on their honeymoon to dampen down their trauma just enough to think they're in what they think is love and then the next generation starts again. *No*, he thought. *No more.*

He leapt out of his seat and the men in black beetle body armor were already behind him. "*Where is she?!*" he shouted and they put what felt like was a bullet in his neck.

He awoke with the bite of the hydraulic hypodermic still throbbing in his jugular, and the smell was what brought it all back to him, a sense memory buried so deeply in his brain that that cocktail of antiseptic and black pepper and cold vent-blown dust made him feel like how he felt as an infant that day, sweet, trusting, and terrified in the same room he was in now, bolted to a chair. There was a series of crude wired hydraulic rings wrapped around his penis.

"We need soldiers," the technician said through her gas mask. The black rib striations of filter at the front covered her face like a car's front grill. Her surgically perfected breasts were exposed, right above where her sanitary full body suit was zippered. She jounced them in her hands and pinched her nipples with distracted, clinical thoroughness. "We're sending you to the front." She turned up a dial and the rings around his penis started inflating and deflating. The electromagnets inside them clicked on and off and they jumped up and down the shaft. The peppery gas started pumping in the room. "We want you to be prepared."

The film on the screen as wide as the room was of dust and sand. Someone tossed a decapitated head to the ground, and the camera came in for a close-up. A woman, her swarthy features obliterated in blood. "This is the future,' a male voice said, and what was presumably his boot smashed down hard on her skull. The video jump-cut to a few moments before the boot came down, and did so again, again, inevitably. Watching the smash so many times in a row made the details stand out, like the pinprick of sound of the matchstick *crack* of what must have been her nose, the way her dark blood-matted hair flew up like waving seaweed, the way a splatter of gore stained the soldier's dusty boot just above the sole every time.

He did not blink. He did not look away. Instead, he stared as intently as he could, searching out every pixel of the image as he inhaled the room's sweet peppery air deeply. *Where is it?* he thought. *Where can it be?* His gaze narrowed in on a desert pebble on the ground, a sand-colored chunk of what could have been shrapnel from a bomb blast. There was the slightest similarity between its pockmarks and the nubbly cellulite of Alice's belly. He took the deepest breath he could and held it and felt its giggly tingle wash over him as he focused in on that pebble, willing it to fill his field of vision as if it was a planet whose surface he was landing upon, making it the hot epicenter of the world around which all other things spin. The machine was tugging him closer to orgasm and he closed his eyes and declared *I will love her, every second of what remains of my life, no matter what they make me do or whether she lives to know it or not. She will glow softly behind every moment*, he thought, as the boot smashed again and again, and on this go-round he noticed the faintest drone of a military helicopter in the soundtrack's distance, and in the staccato baritone beating of its propeller he heard her voice, her beautiful electrolarynxed voice, *the glint in her eyes and the shine in her hair, and the way her face went clean and pure when the chemsex stripped away all her hurt for one perfect moment, writing "with you" on her hand, the taste of peanut butter pie, the sound "Jim," the beating of angel's wings.*

KELBY LOSACK is the author of *Heathenish* and *The Way We Came In*. He lives with his wife in Gulf Coast Texas, where he builds custom furniture and hangs with rappers.

Follow him on Twitter @HeathenishKid

VIOLET LEVOIT is a film critic and novelist. Her work can be found at Turner Classic Movies, Allmovie, Film Threat, and others. She is also the author of five books, including *Scarstruck* and the critically-acclaimed dark Hollywood tale *I Miss the World*. Originally from Baltimore, she lives in Philadelphia.

Instagram: @violetlevoit

JO QUENELL lives in Washington State and writes. Their short fiction has been featured in anthologies and magazines such as *Zombie Punks Fuck Off*, *Dark Moon Digest*, *When the Sirens Have Faded*, and *LAZERMALL*. Their first novella, *The Mud Ballad*, will be released by Weirdpunk Books in Spring 2020.

AXEL HASSEN TAIARI is a writer from Paris, France— but not the fancy parts. His debut novel, *Ruination*, will be released in 2021 by King Shot Press.

www.axeltaiari.com

LYDIA XYTHALI has worked as an EFL teacher and content creator since 2008. Her non-fiction piece "The Kobayashi Maru For Queers" appeared in *Nasty Vol 2*, and she is currently at work on her first novel. She lives in Athens with her husband and an endless supply of homemade hot sauce.

Twitter: @commonlydia
www.lydiaxythali.com